"What was that your superior s included or just no high school girl trembling at the appearance of a guy she has a crush on."

"So you have a crush on me."

"We're not changing the subject. The point is you think you can force me to bend to your wishes with a simple kiss?"

"You think that kiss was simple?"

He was baiting her and she didn't like it.

David took a step forward. There was only a little space between them and he'd just decreased it by half. "Did you forget that you were in my arms? You were part of that kiss, simple or not. You were matching me tongue for tongue."

Images of them kissing, with no space, not even air, between them threatened her resolve. Her stomach felt as if it would turn over or, worse, she'd fall into David's arms as he was suggesting.

He grinned, something she wasn't expecting. "Is it working?" he asked.

"Is what working?"

"Your memory. Your body. Is it pumping passion juice and you want to continue what I started?"

Dear Reader,

Welcome to the first book in my new series, House of Thorn. You'll meet David and watch as he rebuilds a store and a relationship devastated by a major storm. The idea for this book came from a real place along the Atlantic Ocean. I love the sea, the salt air, the sound of the birds. But I know the sea can turn from friend to foe in an instant. This is what happens in *Love in Logan Beach*.

Rosanna Turner fully expected the manager position of Bach's Department Store to fall to her. But a storm took everything she owned, and nearly her life. With David Thorn's arrival, she's sure it will finish her. Rose considers David a privateer profiting from the sorrow of others. Yet his actions prove the opposite and she finds that the storm in her heart is greater than anything Mother Nature could throw at her.

Shirley

LOVE IN LOGAN BEACH

Shirley Hailstock

HARLEQUIN® KIMANI™ ROMANCE

Recycling programs
for this product may
not exist in your area.

ISBN-13: 978-0-373-86515-4

Love in Logan Beach

HARLEQUIN®

Printed in U.S.A.

™ www.Harlequin.com

Shirley Hailstock began her writing life as a lover of reading. She likes nothing better than to find a quiet corner where she can get lost in a book, explore new worlds and visit places she never expected to see. As an author, she can not only visit those places, but she can be the heroine of her own stories. The author of forty novels and novellas, Shirley has received numerous awards, including a National Readers' Choice Award, a Romance Writers of America's Emma Merritt Award and an *RT Book Reviews* Career Achievement Award. Shirley's books have appeared on several bestseller lists, including the *Glamour*, *Essence* and *Library Journal* lists. She is a past president of Romance Writers of America.

Books by Shirley Hailstock

Harlequin Kimani Romance

Visit the Author Profile page
at Harlequin.com for more titles.

To my brother, Eugene, gone too soon. He and I read, watched movies and laughed together. Thanks for the memories. I will always love and miss you.

Chapter 1

David Thorn stood on the seawall in Logan Beach, New Jersey, his arms stretched out. The salty wind blew against his face and the open neck of his white shirt. The Atlantic Ocean stretched from here to the Scottish shores and beyond. Overhead, gulls cawed and swooped to the water in search of today's lunch. David thought about his family vacations in this very spot. And now he would be here daily, working and making the House of Thorn's new Logan Beach store the best he could.

"You're going to work here?" his brother, Blake, shouted with envy over the roar of the waves. "I'd be at the beach every day."

David checked the sky, lowering his arms. It was blue and cloudless, and reminded him of his carefree days as a barefoot boy running through the sand along this beach. David gave his brother a quizzical look. "When you reported the finances, how would you explain your actions to the board?" The board being the family, since Thorn's had always been a family-run business. Their mother started it by selling cakes and pastries out of the family kitchen when her children were barely out of diapers.

Blake looked at the beach. "There is that," he said with a degree of regret in his voice. "I remember some fun days on this beach."

David laughed. "More likely it's the nights you remember. And a certain busty teenager named—"

"Stop." Blake put up his hand. "Let's stay in the present."

Turning around, the two brothers looked at the town. A huge house, now a school, sat in front of them. It had stood there as long as David could remember. Since their vacations here were in the summer, the school was always closed. David wondered what the view was like from the upper floors. Thorn's department store was nowhere near this house, but it too would have a view from the top of the building.

Two floors of the House of Thorn Logan Beach were dedicated to administrative offices and would have full 360-degree views. David believed that sunlight not only fostered production, but also contributed to better attitudes. His law office in Manhattan had huge windows.

The lower floors of the store were dedicated to merchandise.

"Have you reached her yet?" Blake asked, interrupting his thoughts.

"Not yet," he said, shaking his head. He didn't need to ask whom Blake referred to. David had been trying to reach Rosanna Turner for a week, but to no avail.

"I'd forget about her. There have to be other people with experience who can fill her spot."

"I promised the Bachs," David insisted.

"You called her how many times? Twelve? Thirteen? And she doesn't answer, doesn't return your calls. She's probably moved or taken another job. It's not up to you to send out the dogs."

"I'm not calling her again," David said.

Blake smiled. "I knew you'd see reason. That lawyer mind of yours knows when a case is lost."

David didn't reply. And his case wasn't lost. Not yet, David thought to himself, but he wasn't going to debate it with Blake. Promises meant something to David. He'd try one more time, but not by phone. Rosanna Turner had to be somewhere and he'd find her.

They started walking in the direction of the store. It was a couple of miles from the ocean. He could walk it on a good day. Thorn's wouldn't open for at least three more months. The exterior was complete, but the inside needed building, furnishing and stocking. David had relocated from New York City to Logan Beach and secured temporary office space next to the store. He'd toured the construction of Thorn's and spent one day at the shore. He didn't think he'd get many days to spend walking on the sand. Without a boardwalk, Logan Beach still had crowds of sun worshippers dotting the area. While Blake loved the ocean, when David swam, he preferred a pool to the salty sea.

"When do you leave?" David asked his brother when the two reached David's car.

"Next week. I have to go back to New York tonight. My meetings with Dad and Mom take place in the next three days."

When their parents told the family they were planning to retire, David jumped at the chance to take over the conversion of the Logan Beach property. Blake was headed for San Francisco.

David nodded. He remembered the last-minute instructions from his parents before he left for the shore property. Blake's conversation would be different since the San Francisco store was fully operational.

The Logan Beach store needed extensive renovation. And David's first order of business was to find Rosanna Turner and see why she wasn't living up to the person the Bachs had gushed about.

As the sun sat high in the afternoon sky, David parked at the curb and stepped out of his BMW i8. The bluish gray vehicle was incongruously lavish in front of an apartment building whose glory days had probably been before he was born. Punching the lock button on the key fob, he strode around the hood and checked the building's address on his cell phone.

He was in the right place. The structure's door was ajar and unlocked. Three young boys careened out of the opening, laughing in youthful exuberance, and ran toward the main road. David entered. The hall was dark, lit by a single bald bulb that couldn't expend enough light to clear the shadows.

There was no elevator, but a staircase, nearly devoid of paint, led to second and third floors. Rosanna lived in apartment eleven, undoubtedly on the top. Her door had obviously been replaced with a salvaged one. It was a murky yellow against walls that were dark and in need of refinishing.

David knocked.

"Who is it?" someone called.

"David Thorn," he replied, his voice seeming to boom in the empty space.

David thought he heard a sharp intake of breath. A few moments went by before he heard the rhythmic click of several locks being opened.

The door was widened by a few inches and a woman cautiously poked her head through the narrow space, her arms grasping the door in readiness to slam it shut.

"What do you want?" she asked. Her hair was pulled back severely, and she had high cheekbones that showed the hollows of her face. Wearing no makeup, she had the most incredible eyes he'd ever seen—large, brown and watery. He wished she'd smile. He'd like to see how her eyes changed when she did. Her dress was faded and too large, as if she'd recently lost a lot of weight.

"You are Rosanna Turner, right?"

She nodded.

"I'd like to talk to you about Bach's."

"Don't you mean Thorn's?" she asked flatly.

He waited a second before nodding. "I suppose I do."

"Not interested."

She pulled her face back and moved to close the small rectangular opening. David stuck his foot in the door to stop her. It was the first time in his life he could remember doing something so impulsive.

"At least give me a moment to explain why I've been trying to reach you. You haven't answered any of my calls and I've come this far."

Her expressive eyes raked him up and down for a full ten seconds, before she stepped back and allowed him into the apartment. The inside wasn't much better than the outside. It was lit better, due to the large set of windows. The furniture was old, past the comfortable stage, but not as bad as the front door.

"Would you like something to drink—coffee, tea, water?"

He heard no reluctance in her voice and took that as a good sign.

"Coffee would be fine if it's already made."

She didn't say anything, only turned and walked to the small kitchen. The distance couldn't be more than three or four steps from where he stood. David waited, looking through the window. Across the street was an empty lot. The grass was overgrown and several rusted-out garbage cans were strewn throughout the place.

She returned with two mugs. "Cream and sugar?" she asked.

"Black," David told her, turning away from the window. After the light from outside, the room seemed darker. He took the mug and sipped the coffee. It was good.

Rosanna sat down on the out-of-date sofa and David took the seat across from her in a single armchair.

"You're aware that Thorn's has bought the Bachs'

store," he said, stating the obvious, but he needed a way to break the ice. She was cold and his words didn't appear to chip even a sliver of the ice away.

"I'm here to see to the building of the new store and I believe it can be a centerpiece in Logan Beach."

Rosanna looked steadily at him, but she didn't say a word. Both her hands held the coffee cup, yet she did not raise it to her mouth. He wondered what she was thinking. Her quietness unnerved him. David had stood before judges with the worst reputations. He'd stared down criminals and bullies. Yet this underweight woman was making him sweat with her mute stare.

"You were the assistant manager at Bach's."

After a moment she finally said, "It was my last position. I started there as an assistant buyer."

"The Bachs spoke highly of you and your abilities."

Her mouth moved slightly. It was the shadow of the beginning of a smile. Then her expression quickly returned to its original blank stare.

"Are you having a bad day?" David suddenly asked.

The question seemed to get her attention and knock her off center. She set the cup on the table between them.

"No better, no worse than any other day." Her tone was sour.

"Are you working? I mean do you have another job since Bach's?" He didn't think so. It was the middle of the workday and she was home. Her hair and lack of makeup told him she'd been home all day. She might work from home, of course, but there was no evidence of it in the rooms he could see, and that was most of the apartment.

"Yes," she answered coldly. "I work nights."

She offered nothing more. That told him that whatever she was doing, it was below her abilities.

David smiled, hoping she'd see that he was about to offer her something better. He couldn't tell by her expression.

"Do you like your job? Is it satisfying?"

She gazed at him for a moment. "It pays the bills."

She didn't answer his question, but what she said revealed more than an answer would have.

"I'd like you to come back."

"Back to what?"

"To Thorn's."

"I'm not interested in working at Thorn's. The Bachs have sold out. The store is gone. They've moved on, so will I."

David put down his cup and clasped his hands together. He stood up and looked around, then brought his gaze back to her.

"Is that what you're doing?" His voice was stronger, back in his lawyer-addressing-a-witness mode. "It sure doesn't seem so."

The comment brought her out of her seat.

"What do you know about it?" she challenged, her eyes bright and angry.

"Not much," he said. "But I know the person the Bachs talked about, a woman who is competent and efficient, is not the one standing here."

"Get out," she ordered.

His comment angered her. He'd designed it that way. David needed to pull her out of this depression, which seemed to have not only settled on her, but also on every aspect of this room.

"You know nothing about me, nothing about anything. You should try to find out something about the people here before you go blundering into their lives. It hasn't been easy down here since the storm and all the lives that were lost. So why don't you take yourself and your car back to New York and leave us alone."

She'd seen him drive up, he thought. Otherwise, she wouldn't have mentioned the car. David caught the underlying message in her comment. He understood that what his car cost could probably pay for this apartment several times over. He wondered if she had enough food to eat, and it caught him like a blow to his gut. He picked up the coffee cup and drank, unwilling to waste a drop in case she couldn't afford more.

"The storm was like a war," she said. "It changed people. They are no longer the ones they were before it happened."

David should be angry with her attitude, but he admired her spirit. She really felt for the people of Logan Beach and how they were treated.

"I may not know that, and I can't fix everyone who was affected, but there is one person I can help. I can only do one at a time and today it's you." He stopped, letting his words sink in. "I need you to come back and be the assistant manager at Thorn's."

He was careful to choose his words and to let her know this was his store, not a replica of the one she'd left.

"This offer is open for the next twenty-four hours. If you want to stop wallowing in self-pity and return to meaningful employment, my offices are in the building next to the store. Third floor."

He drained his cup and put it down. Then he took a slip of paper with the office address and a business card from his pocket and dropped them on the coffee table.

"I truly hope to see you." He'd lowered his voice to one of concern mixed with sincerity.

Outside her door, David dragged a breath into his lungs. He gripped the stair railing and held it tight enough to splinter the wood. His body was so solidly coiled, he felt only a long run or a hundred laps in a pool would relieve the tension. Rosanna Turner had touched something inside him that roared and he didn't like it. He'd never been in a place so devoid of life, watched a person move through air and not disturb it. David had seen soldiers who were shell-shocked, and Rosanna reminded him of them. He wanted to somehow restore her, force her out of the pattern she'd set and let her know there was a future. This feeling of protection was foreign to him, something he'd never experienced before.

Yet, he'd found the spark of life in her when she accused him of not understanding what had happened to her and the people of Logan Beach. He hadn't been here, had never been in a place where nature had destroyed life and property. He was usually the well-dressed attorney in court, seeking damage restoration for wealthy victims. When working his pro bono cases, which gave him personal satisfaction, they were usually related to personal injury by clients who were financially unable to afford his corporate fees.

David felt bad for treating Rosanna unkindly. His parents didn't rear him that way, but Rosanna needed to be kick-started. It was obvious she'd been pitying herself for a long time and someone needed to let her know that things would not change if she didn't change them.

David hoped that change would begin before the sun rose the next day. He felt Rosanna Turner was more than a depressed woman in a dingy apartment. She only showed a small amount of spark, but David felt it was there and all he needed to do was wait. She would come out of that shell and decide to rejoin the living.

Twenty-four hours would tell him if his theory was true or false.

Rose moved to the window. Sunlight highlighted David's dark hair as he stepped out of the building. He stood a moment, looking first left, then right. She did the same. There wasn't much to see. Several apartment buildings, none of them in great condition, were separated by either demolished buildings or cleared, but overgrown, lots.

The storm had happened two years ago, yet the devastation was still evident. Rose knew about it firsthand.

David moved, catching her attention. He went around his car, shrugged out of his suit jacket, folded it carefully and placed it in the back seat of the luxury car. He opened the driver's door, then looked up. Their eyes connected and Rose jumped back as if she'd been burned.

A moment later, she heard the car door close. The engine purred to life and when she glanced down again, the car accelerated away. Letting out a long, slow breath, she turned away from the windows.

The business card he'd left lay on the table, a small white beacon in a sea of dark wood. She lifted it between two fingers. It bore his New York office address. His cell-phone number had a red circle around it, a signal that he was reachable at any time.

Rose dropped it next to the slip of paper with an address she recognized. It was the building next to the store. While working at Bach's, she'd been in and out of it thousands of times.

Twenty-four hours he'd given her. What would the Bachs think? Should she return? She felt disloyal, even though she knew it was irrational. The final meeting the Bachs held with their employees told them the sale meant Thorn's would keep as many of them as possible. Rose didn't expect to be one of them. She was management and experience told her that new management meant out with the old.

She was the old.

Go back... She heard the words in her head. Go work for the people who had capitalized on someone else's misfortune? It was unconscionable. Rose turned around in a full circle. Every inch of her small apartment could be seen from any place she stood. She'd once been part of the mighty and her fall had been long and hard. David Thorn was offering her a chance to restore some of her former life—if that was possible.

For a moment, the crisis she'd withstood for three

days came back to her. She pushed it away, refusing to allow the thoughts to blossom in her mind.

She needed something more challenging than working nights as a cage cashier in a local casino. But Thorn's!

Could she really go back there, back to the place she'd called home for so many years—a place that was only a shell of what it used to be?

The Jersey coastline stretched for a hundred and thirty miles, from the arm of New York to the tip of Cape May. Logan Beach comprised only twenty of those miles, including five miles of natural preserve.

Rose walked along the water's edge. Holding her loose skirt above her knees, she played footsie with the soft lapping of water.

"Rose." Amber Waverly sang her name and waved as she headed for her. Amber was her best friend. They'd met two years ago under dire circumstances. Together they had saved each other's lives.

Rose waved back and waited for Amber to reach her. Carrying their shoes, Rose and Amber walked slowly. The water was cold, but refreshing.

"Glad to see you out of that apartment. What got you out?" Amber asked.

"David Thorn," she said, emphasizing his name.

"Of the House of Thorn," Amber stated.

"None other." She glanced at her friend.

"How did this happen?"

Rose heard the admiration in her friend's voice. It

irritated her, but Amber never worked at Bach's, so her allegiance lacked.

"He came by my apartment about an hour ago and offered me a job."

Amber hooted. "That's wonderful. You are going to accept it." She stated it as fact without even asking what position he'd offered her. "That night job you have is going nowhere and you know it. You want a future, someplace where you can use your experience and leave your mark."

Amber was a positive person. She had gotten Rose through the storm and she continued to try and push her to return to the retail business.

"I'm having a hard time with it. It's Bach's. The store will have a new name and a new look. Every time I go through the doors, I'll be reminded of how my life changed."

Amber jumped in front of her, took her shoulders and shook her. "Rosanna Turner, what is our motto?"

"Survive, don't let the bad guys win."

"Right."

"The Thorns *are* the bad guys," Rose said, shaking herself loose and continuing to walk.

"You don't know that," Amber responded. "And even if they are, wouldn't it be better to fight the battle from the inside than trying to overcome it from a distance?"

"I'm not sure. I was so looking forward to taking over the store when the Bachs retired. Now I'm relegated back to following orders from a family group with little connection to Logan Beach."

"What did he offer you?"

"Assistant manager."

"That's what you were before. Look at it as an opportunity," Amber said.

"How?"

"Since this is a new store, you can guide it to the place you want it to be. I'm sure David Thorn isn't unreasonable."

"He's a lawyer."

"Lawyer?" Amber repeated.

"I looked him up on the internet. He's a corporate attorney."

"That's perfect." Amber's arm went up to the sky in salute. "If he's into the law and not the retail end of the business, you're sitting in the right seat to get done what you want."

Rose hadn't looked at it like that. Leave it to Amber to see the big picture. Rose disliked her current job. It provided her with a means to eat and pay rent, but did nothing for her ego. She loved retail. David Thorn had offered her an opportunity to return and thoughts of getting back into retail would solve a lot of her problems, but could she let that happen? It was up to her to decide if she wanted to take the leap and turn her life toward a beginning point again, or do something else.

One thing David Thorn's visit forced her to see was that she had to make a move. Her decision had to be whether she'd make it with the House of Thorn or somewhere else.

Chapter 2

The elevator doors slid open silently. Rose raised a foot, but stopped it in midair, allowing it to hang there before her balance tipped her sideways. As the doors began to close, she stepped out. Behind her the elevator closed, cutting off any escape she might want.

Uncomfortable in the heels she'd bought the day before, Rose paused and straightened her new suit jacket. She had only a few things left of her old life. Most were lost in the storm. Her current job didn't require business attire. This was a new Rose. David Thorn's office was at the end of the hall. Already his name was on the door. Rose's stomach clenched. She moved slowly toward it. Without knocking, she opened the carved wooden portal and took in the room.

There were two offices, a reception area and a conference room. No one sat in reception. Nothing lay on the receptionists' desk, indicating no one worked there. A clock on the wall was the only thing in the room that showed any life. The offices sat perpendicular to each other and the doors were open, allowing sunlight from the windows to spill out. To her eyes, the light was blinding.

Hearing the squeak of a chair, she looked toward the sound. David Thorn appeared in the doorway. It was all Rose could do to keep from gasping. She'd forgotten how good-looking he was. Six feet tall, brown eyes with a hint of amusement in them. He was dressed in a gray suit, although behind him she could see his jacket hanging on the back of his chair. She wondered if all he had were suits. He was a lawyer, maybe that's why his wardrobe seemed to be made up of items from Harvé Benard.

She trembled, watching him. The unexpected reaction urging her to run was intense. She wanted more distance between them. She wanted to rush back to her apartment. It might be dark and furnished with second-hand pieces, but it was her sanctuary, a safe place where she could hide from the world.

Standing up taller, Rose reminded herself that she was no longer hiding. She was here. He'd challenged her to come, expecting her to find a reason, rational or not, to remain hidden in that apartment.

"Welcome," David said. "I see you decided to accept my offer."

The harshness of his tone a day ago was still fresh in her mind, although it was missing from today's greeting.

"I didn't have much choice," she said.

"There's always a choice."

Spoken like an attorney. David dealt with choices.

"Let me show you around." David moved toward her. Rose felt trapped. The door had swung closed when she came in, giving her no retreat. She was alone with him. Her heart pounded—she didn't know from what.

Leading her to the second office, the one next to his, he said, "This one is yours."

Rose swept her eyes around the room. It was bright, with a large desk facing the window, a couple of file cabinets and a credenza. The desk held a laptop computer and a printer. All the accessories matched. It was different from the mahogany appointments of her office at Bach's. Rose couldn't help but compare the old with the new.

"Anything you need, order," he said.

Taking her to the conference room ended the short tour.

"Should I start right now?" she asked.

"What about your other job? I assumed you were working."

"I was," she said. "It's finished."

Rose didn't tell him that when she handed in her notice, they had a replacement waiting.

"Then we can begin by touring the facility so you can see the construction."

He left her briefly, going to his own office. He returned with two hard hats. Handing one to Rose, she noticed her name was embossed on it.

"You were that sure I'd come?" she asked, holding the hat with her name facing him.

David looked a little uncomfortable. "I hoped you'd see that coming back was the right thing to do." He paused a moment before continuing. "I want to apologize for yesterday. I didn't come to argue or badger you."

"You were right," she admitted, although it took a lot out of her to tell him that. "I'd been wallowing—I believe that was your word—for a long time. I need to take control of my own life."

David nodded, pushing his hat on his head. "This way," he said.

The walk to the old building, which Bach's had occupied for several generations, was short. The building had a new facade. The Thorns hadn't razed the old structure, one of the few left standing, although it had been severely damaged after the storm. The Bachs decided not to rebuild. They were past retirement age and wanted to spend more time with their grandchildren. Their decision had been a blow to Rose. She was to take over the store as manager when the older couple retired. After the storm, Rose and everyone else were out of jobs and most had sustained huge personal losses.

Rose walked around the first floor of the building. The walls were up. Drywall dust hung in the air. Painters were working in the distance. The ceiling lights were in place, although the ceiling itself was open and unfinished. The huge floor was open, but outlines were in place for certain departments.

"How do you like it?" David asked. He was obviously proud of what he saw. "Chandeliers will be placed along the full length of the room. They're still on order."

Rose's gaze followed his. She imagined the light giving the place a rich look. On the floor were marks detailing the placement of display cases. She stepped onto one of them.

"What's going here?" she asked.

"This is the area designed for fragrances, perfumes, special purchases."

"It's in the wrong place. Perfume counters should be over there." Rose pointed to her left. "Here, people will walk into them. Scarves should be over here." She started walking toward the area. David followed her, but she stopped suddenly and he bumped into her. His hands clasped around her upper arms to steady her.

Rose gasped. The touch of his hands was like fire on her skin. She pointed to a wall, deftly moving away from him. "And where is the children's department?" she asked. "It needs to be over here."

"It's going to be on the third floor. This will reduce the noise level and we plan a full play area for the kids. Safety-wise, it's better for all concerned."

Rose walked quickly to the center of the area, where a sign that read Jewelry had been taped to the floor.

"You can't put Jewelry here?" Rose said, her eyes wide.

"High-end jewelry will be on one side of the aisle and gemstones on the other." David spread his arms to indicate what he meant.

Rose didn't like the changes. The store had been set up for decades one way. Why change it now?

"Rosanna," David said.

She took a long breath, letting it out slowly before turning to face him. She knew he was about to justify this new arrangement.

"I mean this in the best possible way. This is Thorn's, not Bach's. As Bach's it was a wonderful store. It stood in Logan Beach as a staple for over a hundred years. We're not trying to replicate Bach's. They wouldn't appreciate that."

"What are we trying to do?" she asked. Rose was careful to keep her voice level and remove any sarcasm from it. She needed this job and David knew she needed it. He was going to be the person she reported to, so she should act like an employee. Why she wasn't, she didn't know. She did know, however, that the places on her arms where he'd touched her were still smarting and her heart had yet to return to a normal rhythm.

"We've tested this layout in other Thorn stores and it's a scientific approach to crowd flow. Moving from one area to another is easier and usually in line with buying patterns. Those people who buy suits go on to purchase shoes and blouses."

"I'm sure this has worked in other places, but you need to be aware how important it was for people here to return to things that are familiar."

David took her arm and walked her away from the earshot of the workmen. Again Rose felt the electrical shock of his touch.

"Rosanna, as you told me, the hurricane happened. It's not like people don't know that or don't want to put it behind them. Don't you want to put it behind you?"

She hadn't been prepared for that question. She turned away from him as memories rushed into her mind. David came up behind her before she had time to formulate an answer.

"I'm not asking that you forget it or pretend it didn't happen," he said. "It changed people. I get that. But if you plan to stay in Logan Beach, then you have to be willing to accept the change."

"We are accepting the change," she said tightly. "We have no choice but to accept it. The people of Logan Beach have been through a crisis and they feel comfortable knowing that some things are the same, comfortable."

David moved around to face her. "I do understand. And I can't undo what's happened. No one is the same. Starting over shows the renewal of life."

Hating to have her own words thrown in her face, Rose remained quiet.

David dropped his shoulders as if in defeat. "Rosanna, trust me. When the store opens, people will be happy to see something new. They'll welcome the fact that we didn't try to duplicate Bach's."

Rose hunched and dropped her shoulders. She had no choice in this matter. Thorn's owned the building and everything that went with it. All that would happen to her would be that she'd be out on the street again. But as for trusting him? That was something she couldn't do. She could accept changes in the store. She had ideas for the better placement of departments. She'd never written any of them down, but her plan had been that when the Bachs retired and left her in charge, she would restructure some of the areas. The difference between her and David was she would have done them a few at a time.

David was ripping the bandage off in one swift snap.

But then wasn't that how she removed bandages?

Those beautiful eyes glanced up from the computer screen when David knocked on Rosanna's door. They were light brown and *foretelling* was the only word he could use to describe them. She wore makeup today, not like when he'd surprised her by pushing into her apartment. It highlighted her eyes to the point of mesmerizing.

"You must be tired of reading papers and screens."

"Some of it is interesting," she said.

"Shut it down. That's enough for today. Come on, let's get out of here."

Her expression didn't change as she glanced at her arm, looking for the time, but there was no watch there. Angling her head, she checked the clock on the wall in the reception area. He looked in the same direction. It was three o'clock and she'd been at it for hours. Boring hours, if David thought about it, although he didn't really know her background or her temperament, only that she wasn't thrilled that the Thorns had taken over Bach's.

"Coffee?" he asked.

"I'd love a cup."

"There's a quaint little bakery not far from here. We could get some coffee there."

"I'm familiar with it," she said.

Of course she was, David thought as they headed out. She'd worked in this area for years. She probably knew everything about it and the whole of Logan Beach.

David had known it as a bakery in his youth. Now it was a coffee house with some baked goods. They served at least twenty types of coffee, a variety of teas and a few pastries.

"What would you like?" David asked as they approached the counter.

"Plain coffee," she said.

"Black? Cream and sugar?" he asked.

"I'll add them," she answered.

David waited until she'd added a drop of cream and two sugars to her cup before speaking.

"Don't think of this as an interview or anything," he said. "The job is already yours, barring any unforeseen circumstances. I thought we could use this time as a sort of getting-to-know-you exercise."

"Getting to know you?" she queried.

He nodded. "Like the Miss America candidates do. I know you can't live around here and not know all the details about that contest."

Atlantic City was only half an hour from Logan Beach. The annual beauty contestants sometimes spilled into Logan Beach for photo shoots.

"I'll start," David told her. He understood she was apprehensive. He was technically her boss and he knew the dynamics that came into play when a person didn't know the reason for the meeting.

"I was a summer resident here. My uncle used to

rent a house and bring my brothers and me along with his sons here for a month."

"So you're not a stranger to the area?"

She gazed at him, cradling her coffee cup in both hands as if she needed it to warm her. Her voice held surprise that he was familiar with the city.

"I haven't been here in a couple of years, but I used to come every summer, even while I was in law school." Logan Beach wasn't that big, even though it had a long coastline. Yet David had never run into her. He'd been in the Bach's store. As a member of a family running department stores, he couldn't go anywhere and not check out the competition. It was a family requirement. He wondered if his reports about Bach's had interested his parents in the store once it was for sale.

"Most people come here for the beach. Is that what attracted your family?" Rosanna asked.

"I think it was just a place to let five boys run wild." He laughed, but Rosanna didn't. "How did you get here?"

"I was born in Logan Beach."

No elaboration. David was used to people continuing to talk, more than they should in some cases.

"Any siblings?"

"Only child."

"Were you a lonely only child?" he asked pointedly.

Rosanna stared at him. "No. My life was filled with friends and activities."

"What kind of activities?" He was trying to get her to talk, to open up. It was on the tip of his tongue to ask about dance lessons, sports, anything young girls would do, but thought that would elicit another one-word answer.

"The normal ones—tennis, horseback riding at Island Beach, roller blading, gymnastics, swimming, dances, cotillions and proms."

"Do you still ride and play tennis?"

"Sometimes."

"Maybe we can have a company league and play regularly."

"Would you like me to add that as an employee recreational option?"

He shook his head. "We're going to have a lot to do and when our human resources department is up and running, they can work on that. But we're not here for work."

"Yes." Rosanna's head bobbed up and down. "The getting-to-know-you meeting."

"It's not a meeting."

She took a drink of her coffee. David thought it must be cold by now.

"Would you like a fresh one?" he asked.

She shook her head. "We lived across from the beach. My carefree days were spent with friends, swimming and going to parties. I went to college in Atlanta—Clark Atlanta University. I majored in business finance and minored in music."

Music, he thought, but didn't say anything. She'd finally begun to speak in sentences of more than one word and he didn't want to stop her with questions.

"When I returned home, I got a job with a brokerage house in Philadelphia. I hated the commute. One day I saw an ad for a job in the finance department at Bach's. I got it and expressed an interest in being a buyer. Mrs. Bach took me aside and taught me the ropes. From there I advanced to assistant manager."

Rosanna had delivered the speech as if she was reciting her résumé.

"During college, other than being an A student, what did you do?"

She looked at him. "How do you know I was an A student?"

"Something about you says it. And the Bachs gave you a glowing recommendation."

"Well, I wasn't an A student."

"Then you were a fun student. What did you do for fun?"

She smiled. She must have remembered something.

"That's it," he said.

"What?"

"You smiled. I've been hoping you would."

"What?" she asked again.

"I believe that's the first time I've seen you smile since we met."

"Sorry, it won't happen again."

David stared at her, then saw her straight face turn into a small smile. "So you do have a sense of humor."

"Did you think I lost it in the storm?" Again Rosanna's face had only the shadow of a smile on it, but David realized she was kidding.

"One day maybe I'll get a full, unadulterated laugh."

"I'll work on it," she said.

* * *

"So, how was your first day?" Amber asked, pouring them both a glass of wine.

Rose accepted hers and curled her bare feet under her as she sat on Amber's sofa. The two women had met during the storm's crisis and shared the same makeshift hospital tent. The experience bonded them as if they'd been friends from birth.

"Exhausting," Rose answered. "I needed a hard hat to tour the store."

"A tour conducted by Mr. Thorn, I take it?"

Her glib tone was unmistakable, especially as it was followed by a Cheshire-cat smile and a fluttering of her eyelids as she took a sip of her wine.

Rose nodded, taking a sip of her own drink.

"So, spill, how was he? Is he as good-looking as his photo?"

"Photo? What photo?" she repeated.

"I looked him up on the internet. Apparently, the entire family is made up of gorgeous guys."

Rose had looked up the Thorns, too. She'd seen David's photo, maybe the same one Amber was referring to. She hadn't even made the decision to accept David's offer until she left the casino in the early morning hours.

"He's tall, around six feet. Dresses and acts like a lawyer."

"Don't compare him to the Bachs. They're bound to have different management styles."

Rose rolled her eyes. "They do. He's changing everything. The store won't be recognizable."

"It'll be a House of Thorn's store," Amber said.

Rose took another sip of her wine. Amber was a realist and didn't pull punches. She said what came to her mind. David came to Rose's mind. She wondered what photo Amber had seen. David had a power that surrounded him. You immediately knew he was in control. He was a decision maker. She could imagine him in court, arguing before a jury and convincing them that his point of law was the correct and only decision they could come to.

"Thinking about him?"

Amber's question caught her off guard.

"Who?" she asked, but they both knew the answer to that.

Amber frowned, screwing her face up in an exasperated expression.

"I wasn't," Rose lied. "I was thinking about the building layout." She wasn't thinking about the store, but the strange conversation they'd had in the bakery.

"That's your story…" Amber left the rest of the cliché hanging. "You are going back tomorrow, *right*?"

Rose signed and nodded. "I've spent too many years in retail that I don't know how to do anything else."

"You could learn," Amber told her.

"I feel like I'm starting all over again anyway. They might as well put me in the mailroom."

Amber sat forward. Placing her glass on the coffee table, she looked directly at Rose. "We're strong. We'll survive. We can do anything. We're invincible," Amber said, reciting one of the mantras they'd said over and over during the storm.

Rose smiled. "Yes, we can," she said. "But maybe not in a casino making change."

Both women laughed.

When Rose arrived the next morning, she was wearing gray pants and a green blouse with a dark green jacket. The outfit looked like a suit, but Rose had put it together.

In the middle of her desk was a large white envelope with her name on it. Opening it, she found employment forms, insurance papers, a W-9 form, a confidentiality form and a notice about security cameras.

"I should have given these to you yesterday," David said from where he stood in her doorway. "They're a formality, but they must be filed to make everything legal."

Rose nodded. David took a step into the office. "There's another envelope," he said.

Rose picked up the white, legal-size envelope. It was sealed and had nothing except the return address of the store in the corner. She opened it and inside was an offer letter and a signing bonus check. Rose's eyes widened when she saw the amount. She hadn't seen that much money since the Christmas bonus from the Bachs three years ago. Mist rushed to her eyes and she forced herself not to cry.

Rose wondered if David knew what this check meant to her. She wore borrowed clothes and subsisted on simple food. It wasn't that she hadn't tried to find other employment, but since the storm there were few places to work. Her savings were practically gone and she hadn't known what would happen when her bank account reached zero. If David Thorn wasn't standing in her doorway, she'd break down and cry. Forcing herself to remain calm, she looked up at him.

"Thank you," she whispered. Emotion kept her voice from its normal level.

She looked down at the forms, expecting David to leave her alone to fill them out. Instead he took the chair in front of her desk. Rose looked at him expectantly.

"You can fill those out and give them back to me next week. Right now, I have something for you to do."

"All right," Rose said. Her duties hadn't been spelled out and she looked forward to having a purpose.

"I thought about what you said yesterday when we were touring the store."

"I was out of line—" she began.

David raised his hand to stop her apology. Rose heeded his warning and stood waiting.

"First, I'd like you to forget how things used to be." David paused, but Rose decided not to challenge the remark. "If you could design the store of your dreams, if you could start from scratch and do whatever you wanted, what would your store look like?"

Rose had to think about that. "You want an answer now? Off the top of my head?"

"Not every nail and wall-color choice, just what would it look like?"

Rose thought for a long moment. Pushing the envelope aside, she searched for paper. Inside a drawer, she found a yellow legal pad and pulled it out. She began drawing squares to indicate areas of the floor. She chose the bridal department to begin with. David watched her. Between them was a desk light. He looked over it and bobbed his head several times as he followed her train of thought.

"Lights would be here to showcase the display case."

He got up and moved around, pulling his chair so he sat next to her.

Rose felt all the air in the room leave it. She felt the heat of his body, smelled the aftershave he used. Her eyes closed a moment and she took in the erotic nature of it. David asked a question, drawing her back to the task. She didn't hear it.

"What was that?" she asked.

"What is in this area?" He used his finger to circle a large open area.

Rose drew a 3-D circle. "This is where the bride stands to show off her dress." Drawing basic lines at right angles to represent chairs, and arches to represent a walkway, she said, "The bride comes down this aisle and steps onto the pedestal. Any family or friends with her will see her in a ceremony setting."

"I like it," he said.

His hand dropped on her shoulder. Rose's throat went dry and she could feel the heat of his touch through her suit jacket and blouse, searing into her skin.

"Maybe we'll give some of this to the designer and see what she thinks."

A knife plunging into Rose's gut would have felt better than his words. These were her thoughts. She hadn't expected him to take them and give them away. She pushed the pad toward him in a dismissive manner.

He got what he wanted, now someone else could take over the business of putting it together, changing it to their way of thinking. Rose expected nothing to be the same as her vision of the department.

"We haven't really gone over my duties yet," she said.

"You're the assistant manager. I suppose your duties are the same as they were under the Bachs."

"That was a fully stocked store with employees already hired. I dealt with buyers, personnel, shipping, mail order, budgets, payroll, everything the Bachs didn't handle."

"You can do the same here."

"That's an open catalog," Rose said.

"If you need help, hire someone. You're the assistant manager," he repeated.

Cocking her head, Rose scrutinized David Thorn. She didn't know him, didn't understand his motives. She wondered if he was really trusting her, or if he wanted to see what she would do with the authority he gave her. She'd had this job before and she was comfortable with it. She could do whatever the store needed.

And she'd prove it.

David left for the day wondering about Rosanna. As he pulled his car into the rush hour traffic, Rosanna was still on his mind. She remained an enigma to him. Usually he read people easily. He'd been trained to observe them, get at the underlying causes of problems or secrets they held. But with her it was like trying to open an oyster with a toothpick.

He hadn't realized where he was driving and when

he saw the small sign reading Legal Aid Office, David stopped. He hadn't met any lawyers since he arrived in Logan Beach and this was a perfect time.

Inside, the place was crowded, even at six o'clock in the evening. The office seemed to accommodate those who couldn't come during the nine-to-five workday.

"May I help you?" asked a large woman wearing a bad wig. She sat behind a high desk and looked him up and down in a gesture that said he didn't appear to look like the usual people who come to a legal-aid office.

"I'm an attorney and stopped by to say hello and introduce myself." He handed her his card.

She glanced at it and then up at him. "House of Thorn," she said. "Isn't that the new store that's going up across town?"

"It is."

"Are you representing them in some action?"

"No, I guess I wasn't very clear. I'm not introducing myself as someone's lawyer."

"Then are you here to help?" she asked.

David hadn't thought of helping. He'd just come to meet other colleagues in his profession. But the question caught him off guard.

"I don't think I can. I am with the store, just didn't know any other lawyers in Logan Beach. How many work here?"

"Not nearly enough," she said as a man approached the desk. "Perfect timing. Paul, meet Mr. Thorn of the House of Thorn. He's a lawyer and wants to meet some other lawyers. This is Paul Varga—he runs the place."

The two shook hands. "Are you here to volunteer?"

"I take it you're shorthanded," David said, since he'd been asked the same question within two minutes of entering the building.

"Very."

"I'd like to help you out, but my hands are full right now."

"Well, maybe some time in the future. Stop by anytime. We can always put you to work."

Someone came up to Paul and his attention was gone. David realized he'd been dismissed. It wasn't something that happened to him often. Paul was busy. People called to him from every direction. There wasn't much time to talk to someone not willing to help.

David nodded to the woman behind the desk and left the building. He slipped into the driver's seat, but didn't start the engine. His office in New York was clean and tidy, with law books and a waiting room. This place was little more than a warehouse with mismatched chairs and working men and women waiting for a straw of help.

He needed to help. David felt the calling of his profession. He knew Thorn's was his priority. Things were going well and they were on schedule, but there was a lot of overseeing to do. He couldn't possibly leave everything to Rosanna.

Reaching for the ignition, he stopped, his finger on the start button. He didn't press it, but took his foot off the brake and opened the car door.

Chapter 3

Rose stayed in her office long after David had gone. There were two ways she could interpret David's comments about giving her preliminary plan to the designers. She could let it go and have them redo the floors to their desire. Or she could present her own version of what the House of Thorn Logan Beach should look like. The idea was practically resolved in her mind before she finished formulating it.

Thank goodness it was Friday. She had the weekend to create her model. Longer than that, and her window of opportunity might close.

It took her the entire weekend to complete, as she started working late at night on Friday, and finished up on Monday morning before going to work. She had both a 3-D computer simulation of the entire store and a physical model of the first three floors.

Getting the model to the office was a precarious trip, but she arrived without a mishap. Setting it up in the conference room, along with her laptop, she covered the model, then made a cup of coffee and went over her presentation before David arrived.

Even though she heard the door of the office open and close, his presence at the conference room door surprised her.

"What's this?" he asked, coming into the room.

"I want to show you something, but get your coffee and settle first."

She knew he had no appointments.

At least he hadn't mentioned any. David was good about keeping her up-to-date and letting her know when he was leaving the office.

"I had coffee on the way in."

"Then sit down. I have something I want to present."

He entered the room, taking a seat near the computer and across from her.

"One of the comments you made last week was to ask me what I would do if the store was completely mine and I could design it the way I wanted it."

Glancing at David, she wanted to know what he was thinking. Her heart beat a little faster and she knew it wasn't due to her being nervous about her presentation. Each time she saw him her body did things that surprised her, things she knew shouldn't happen.

David nodded for her to continue.

"This is a computer rendering of the six retail floors."

Her voice was several notes higher than normal. She took a moment to clear her throat.

She tapped a key on the computer and the entire outside facade of the store was projected on the screen at the end of the polished conference table.

David faced the screen, sitting forward in his seat.

"This may not be your vision of the store, but I wanted to start at the beginning."

There were large display windows with miniature models in them wearing the latest summer fashions. Rose's 3-D model had real dolls she found in a thrift store.

David nodded, but didn't give an opinion.

She went on. Every few minutes, as she added more and more floors to the store and explained where everything would be placed and how the lighting would display it, David nodded. He asked a question now and then. She tried to read his expression, but he had his lawyer face on.

Rose continued. She was proud of the design. When she got into the project, she found it didn't tire her out. It inspired her. When the Bachs retired, her plan was to change some of the departments, but with Thorn's she had a blank slate. She visited the other stores online, incorporating some of the recurring layouts and creating others. She thought about crowd flow and the natural movement of people from one department to another.

David had said it was scientific and she kept that in mind as she completed her presentation.

"I've made a mock-up of the first three floors," she said when she finished the computer simulation.

Unveiling the three-dimensional model, she stood behind it. David came around to look at it.

"Is this done to scale?" he asked, his first question in a long time. She heard the awe in his voice and didn't know if it meant he approved or was just surprised.

"You must have worked for days on this."

"Just the weekend," she said, keeping to herself the number of hours she'd put in. Unfortunately, she yawned at that moment, putting her hand up to stifle it and hoping he didn't see it.

David turned the model around, perusing it from every angle. He stooped down, leveling his eye with the model.

"This is beautiful. You should have told me you were an artist."

He glanced at Rose and she smiled, yet she didn't want to be complimented on the art. She wanted him to like the layout, approve the design and at least let some of it be used.

"If I approve this, do you think, among your duties, you can work with the designers to implement it?"

Rose blinked, unsure of what she'd inferred.

"Are you giving me approval?" Her voice was more tentative than she would have liked it to be.

"Not yet." He shook his head. "Email me a copy of the proposal and I'll present it to the Board and get back to you."

Rose's face fell, but she quickly lifted her chin and looked David square in the eye. She knew what his comment meant. He needed time to find a reason to reject it.

She knew it was good—better than good—but it wasn't created by the House of Thorn or any of their agents.

"Don't get me wrong, Rosanna. It's a great design."

Rose nodded absently. "What about the designers?"

"I wish I'd met you before I hired them. I could have saved the family a lot of money."

Rose smiled for real then.

"One thing," he said.

She froze, feeling like "here it comes."

"The outside of the building."

"Yes?" she prompted.

"Because of the previous storms, we've committed to shoring up the foundation. The windows are made of special glass that can resist hurricane-force winds. The building, while it will have the look of the other Thorn stores, will be different than what you have here."

Rose nodded. "That sounds like a good thing."

"And the lettering of the logo." He put his finger on the word *Thorn's*.

Rose smiled. "I couldn't find the right font."

"I'll have to pass this by the board, my family, and see what they think," he repeated.

Rose's heart hammered and her face burned as if she was on a hot beach, but she was pragmatic. Board, she thought. Even if they were his family, they would never approve a project already in progress, one they'd laid out money for a team of designers to complete. She'd been excited for a moment, but now she knew she didn't stand a chance. It didn't matter that hers was better, she'd wasted time and energy thinking David would even seriously consider it. Still, in the back of her mind, she held out a tiny amount of hope.

"I can fix that logo before you go if you know the font name," she said evenly.

"I'll find out and let you know."

He stood up from his crouched position.

"Good job, Rosanna."

"Rose," she said. "My friends call me Rose."

"Rose," he repeated, his voice barely above a whisper, yet it seemed to roar in her mind.

The benefit of the doubt. Rose heard a message her father used to give her when she was young and he'd take her to his office. When there was a problem related to people, he advised her to always give them the benefit that they might be right, or at least have a viable reason for whatever the issue was.

So she was going to believe that David had given her proposal its due when he presented it to the board.

Rose yawned. It has been a long weekend. Blinking, she tried to focus on the task list that appeared to grow with each ticking minute. Getting up, she headed for the kitchenette. She poured what had to be her hundredth cup of coffee in the last seventy-two hours. When she returned there was a note on her desk.

She picked up the white piece of paper and read out loud the three words on it.

"Go for it."

With the paper still in her hand, she went into David's office. She needed to know what it meant. It had only been an hour since she'd finished presenting. How could he have called a meeting, even if it was with family, and have a decision this fast?

"What does this mean?" Rose asked, extending her hand with the note in it.

David smiled. "You have a go."

Rose said nothing for a moment. She was stunned.

"H-how?" she stammered. "I mean when? There wasn't enough time." She stopped because she was rambling. Her mind was rambling.

"I called the board. Or rather I emailed them. They said any changes I wanted to make were my decision."

Rose's mouth dropped open as the full impact of what she was hearing processed in her brain. Clamping her hand over her mouth, Rose kept herself from screaming.

"I can see that makes you happy," David said. "Your eyes are as bright as the sun."

Rose stifled a laugh. It came out as almost a sneeze.

"I'm sorry," she apologized.

"No need. I know exactly how you feel."

Rose nodded and as she headed toward her office, she knew he couldn't possibly understand how she felt. She stopped and looked at the ceiling, but she was really looking to the heavens. Closing her eyes, she whispered a prayer. "Thank you, Daddy," she said.

Standing there for several seconds, she thought about David. He wasn't as bad as she initially thought. Maybe it was his family and not him who'd bought Bach's. That thought brought her out of her reverie and she moved.

She should have been riding on air. David had just given her the go-ahead, but she'd been living on adrenaline and coffee for a few days. Returning to her office, she sat down and suddenly a long weekend of pushing herself to create and finish in time to present her ideas slammed into her like a sprinting runner bent on getting to the front of the pack.

At her desk, she rested her head and closed her eyes a moment. Sleep stole over her in seconds...

Her chair slid backward, crashing against the wall and jerking her awake.

David yanked her door open and rushed inside.

"Are you all right?" he asked, concern evident in his voice.

Rose was still trying to get her bearings and didn't immediately focus on him. So she was unprepared when he pulled her chair around and went down on one knee so he was level with her.

Rose tried to keep the distress from her face, but she was too tired.

"I'm all right," she said. "Just a little tired."

"You're going home," David announced. His don't-argue-with-me voice penetrated her mind, but she ignored it.

Pushing back, she said, "I don't need to go home. I have a ton of things to do and with the addition of the—"

"Every one of them can wait until tomorrow. You've worked the entire weekend, night and day, it appears, so you're going home."

Rose accepted the argument. The thought of taking a nap seemed like the best idea in the world. But she didn't want him to think she was incapable of handling her responsibilities.

David must have read her expression, because he answered her concern as if she'd voiced it.

"No one will think ill of you for taking a comp day. We all need them now and then."

There was no one except the two of them, but Rose didn't point that out. She nodded and moved to stand, but he was directly in her path. David got up and his hand went under arm, helping her to her feet. Rose felt steadier than she had before he appeared in her office, but she didn't protest his touch. It was warm and she wanted to put her hand over his and turn to face him. Stifling the urge, she stood and pulled away, using the need to gather her purse and briefcase as a reason to remove the contact between their two bodies.

Logan Beach wasn't a large place, even though its population swelled in the summer to thousands.

"Is it all right if I ask you a question?" Rose asked when they were driving in his car.

"Sure."

"You're a trained lawyer. How did you come to manage the Logan Beach store? Wasn't the New York legal scene more your style?"

David negotiated around a tractor trailer and made a left turn before speaking. "About a year ago, my parents called a family meeting. There are five of us. My two brothers and twin cousins. The twins were raised by my parents and are more like brothers than cousins. Our parents announced their retirement."

"Ah," Rose commented.

"It wasn't going to happen that fast. My mother is a visionary. She started out as a stay-at-home mom, but wanted more to life than rearing children. She loved to cook. So she started selling cakes from her kitchen in DC."

"DC? I thought you were from New York."

"No," David said. He stopped at a light and glanced at Rose. She didn't look as tired as when he'd found her asleep at her desk. "We moved to New York after she started baking. My father was transferred there and she had a few clients in Washington who recommended her to stores in New York. That was the beginning. Eventually the business grew so that she had to move production out of our house and into a small store, where she added ice cream and cold drinks to her menu."

David remembered those days. He loved the ice cream.

"Soon it was evident she needed help. We all helped out after school and in the summer, but we were probably eating more than we sold."

Rose laughed at that.

"My father quit his job when the store was making more profits than he made as a retail salesman. And he was tired of always traveling, especially after his brother died suddenly and my twin cousins came to live with us."

"Oh, I'm so sorry."

David felt the depth of emotion in her words. She must have lost loved ones, too.

"That must have been hard on you as a family."

"It was, but I think because we had one another—we got through the grief faster than those who have no one." Before he realized what he'd said, the words were out. He wasn't sure if Rose had anyone, but he didn't get the impression that she did, at least no one close. And so many people were going through the same trauma as she was.

"Go on," Rose prompted. "How did you get from a baked-goods store to a department chain?"

"My uncle left a small retail business that my father took over. People in the retail store would ask about ordering from the bakery and my father would take their orders and pass them on. It was my mother who came up with the idea of putting a bakery in the retail store, giving people a one-stop-shopping experience."

"Good idea," Rose said. "That's a staple of the House of Thorn."

"Every Thorn store has a bakery. The idea proved to be a perfect arrangement. After a while the bakeries were doing equal business with the retail store. My parents decided to open more stores, one at a time until, in addition to the original bakery, they had five stores in as many states and my father was back on the road, managing them."

"So did you decide to help out by managing the new Logan Beach store?"

He shook his head. "That's where the family meeting came into play."

Rose leaned her head back on the seat, her neck rolling until she faced him. He felt a small twinge of awareness under her scrutiny.

"When the twins went to college, my parents announced they planned to retire after the twins graduated. They would stay in business until then. After that they planned to go on an around-the-world cruise and the empire would pass to the next generation."

"So obviously the twins graduated."

"Two years ago."

He looked at her. Her eyes were closed, but they opened, looking directly into his. David turned back to concentrate on the traffic.

"When they asked which stores we wanted to manage, I chose this one."

"Why?"

"I love Logan Beach. All my memories here are fond ones. I expect to make more in the future."

The drive from the store to Rose's apartment was only twenty minutes. Their conversation hit a lull and when David glanced at her again, she'd fallen asleep. He smiled at her and pulled her head against his shoulder.

David drove slowly, not wanting to wake her. He also wanted to prolong the drive. He couldn't believe what she'd done with the plans for the store. The design was better than good. Smiling to himself, he thought of their argument over the placement of display cases, and the best method of directing the flow of customers, yet she'd incorporated it into her design. It wasn't a battle or a war that he'd won, but he felt it was a crack in the glass case she'd protected herself with.

Pulling up in front of her apartment, David cut the engine and looked sideways. Rose didn't move. He leaned over and released her seat belt. She fell against him.

Her breath was warm on his neck and he didn't immediately move back or push her head away. He turned his face slightly, taking a more comfortable position, one that was a prelude to his mouth seeking hers.

David stopped himself. He knew if he moved another inch he'd kiss her, and while the thought was foremost in his mind, the timing was wrong.

"Rose," he whispered.

She stirred, yet remained asleep.

"Rose," he said again, this time his voice a little stronger.

Her eyes opened and she looked up. It only took a moment for her to realize where she was. Quickly, she pushed back and shifted in her seat.

David knew she would react that way, yet he'd hoped she wouldn't.

"Excuse me, I must have dozed off. I guess I'm more tired than I thought." She glanced out the window. "We're here."

"I'll see you in."

"There's no need of that," Rose insisted.

"You were asleep in seconds. I want to make sure you get to your apartment safely." He didn't wait for her to agree or disagree. He was out of the car and coming around to her side. The truth was, he wanted to make sure she got safely inside.

The hallway was still dim, but his eyes adjusted quickly. He followed her up the steps and stopped at her door.

"I'll be in tomorrow," she said.

David nodded. He knew there was no reason to argue. And he didn't want to.

"I won't be in until noon," he told her.

"Oh." She frowned. "I don't remember anything on the schedule."

"It's not there," David said. "I'll be at Legal Aid to see how I can help out. I promise I'll get back in time to take care of whatever is on my schedule."

"No worry," Rose said.

"I won't. I'm sure you can handle anything that comes up."

In the ensuing week, David watched Rose as she moved like a dynamo. She was on the phone talking to designers, incorporating her plans into the ones they'd presented. Her office was a collection of charts, fabrics, color schemes and her endless lists of things to do.

He loved seeing her busy. He loved watching her move. In fact, it was hard for him to keep his eyes off her.

Rose had posted a large magnetic whiteboard in the reception area that showed their locations at a glance. Seeing her name on it each morning when he arrived added a lift to his day. He wondered what she did when she wasn't in the office. Did she ever think of him the way he was thinking of her?

Their relationship had begun like two sharp rocks on a beach, but the water was slowly wearing away the edges. It was only a short time ago that David had met a fiercely independent woman who was in no way like the efficient executive who spoke with a strong voice to suppliers, gave directions to the builders and had fallen asleep on his shoulder.

Even though he'd given Rose the go-ahead and she was deep into details, on Friday he went to her office with news from the board of directors. Her head was down and she was concentrating on a floor plan. She looked up. The light hit her face at just the right angle. Her liquid brown eyes were large and fringed with long lashes—the perfect setting. David remembered that her eyes were the one thing that arrested his attention the day he met her. Today, he could drown in them.

"David, you're staring," she said. "Do I have lipstick on my nose?" Her hand went to her nose and she wiped at it and looked at her fingertips.

He cleared his throat and shook his head, blinking to pull himself out of the stupor he'd fallen into.

"Sorry, I was thinking of something." He tried to cover himself, because his thoughts were only of her. "I brought you some good news."

She smiled tentatively and David had to force himself to concentrate on why he was here.

"I sent your plans for the store to my brothers, who'll be managing stores in California and New York, and my cousins, who'll have stores in the Midwest and Texas. They liked your ideas and will implement some in their stores."

Rose smiled widely. "You're kidding me?"

"Not in the least," he said, shaking his head. She had a beautiful smile. And she used it more often these days than she had in the beginning. David felt she was losing the shell she had around her. "One of them wants you to consult…" He paused, gauging her reaction. Her smile grew even wider. "I told him one job at a time, but the final answer is up to you."

"Your answer was right." She glanced around the crowded room. "There are so many details here and I need to work with the builders and suppliers on a daily basis."

"He didn't mean now. We want the different stores to reflect the areas where they are, but some of the details are the same."

"The branding is there," Rose said. "When someone enters a House of Thorn store, they know where they are. I'd love to help, but only after this store is complete if he can wait that long."

"The store is complete now, but every few years there need to be changes to keep customers interested." David didn't tell her that he didn't want her that far away.

"So they can wait?" she asked.

"You enjoy this," he said, not answering her question.

"More than I thought I would. I had some ideas for changes that I would make when the Bachs retired, but this is so much bigger. I got to begin with a clean slate, a completely empty floor, and I could design it any way I wanted. Building that model was a work of love."

David watched the animation on her face. She was passionate about this project. He understood her feeling. It was the way he felt when he won a case for a client who really deserved justice—usually someone who couldn't pay for his services.

"And to see it come to life…" Rose trailed off. "I'm

sorry," she apologized. "I'm running away with myself. You must have things to do."

He did, but he'd much rather listen to her. Then his phone rang. David pulled it out of his pocket and looked at the display. His mother's photo appeared in the small screen. He glanced up at Rose.

"Go on. Take it," she said. She stood up, picking up her hard hat. "I have to go to the store."

Coming around the desk, she preceded him through the door.

Her perfume lingered.

David closed his eyes and breathed in.

When David was leaving for the day, Rose was still in her office. He poked his head in the doorway and said good-night. She'd developed a routine for the two of them. When she wasn't in the office, she was at the store seeing how the construction was coming. He could check her location on the magnetic whiteboard. He'd given her free rein with the store makeover and she was adding tasks to her plate based on what needed to be done.

The office building had a small parking lot and sometimes his was the only car left—despite David noticing that she always left after he did. Tonight he was waiting to make sure she got home safely. As he suspected, she left the office and started walking. He knew where she lived and it had to be five or six miles from the store. How had she arrived in the last week? Had she walked?

David pulled the car up to her and stopped. Rosanna looked around and did a double take.

"You don't have a car?" he called, getting out of his BMW.

"I use walking as an exercise," she explained.

"You always exercise carrying a briefcase?" David challenged, indicating the weight in her hand.

She looked down at the case as if she'd only just remembered it was there.

"I didn't need a car tonight. I'm meeting someone."

"Who?" The word came out without thought.

Her eyes widened. They were expressive and David loved looking into them. Of course, he held himself in check every time he did.

"Isn't that a little personal?" she asked.

"It could be, but I don't want anything happening to you. You don't live in the best area." He added the last statement to take away the implication that he felt more than concern for an employee.

"It's broad daylight." She glanced at the sky.

"Where are you meeting this friend? I'll give you a ride."

"All right," Rose said.

David opened the passenger door and held it. She handed him the briefcase and slid into the low seat. Walking around, he put the case on the back seat and got behind the wheel.

"Where are we going?"

"The Grogg. It's a little pub on Seaman's Way. I'll direct you."

David drove and Rose said very little other than to tell him where to turn.

"You've been here awhile now. Is everything going all right?" he asked, using small talk to break up her role as navigator.

"I'm slowly getting the hang of it."

"Did you decide to hire some help?"

"Not yet. I'm feeling my way through. I have enough to keep another person busy, but I don't have time to train anyone yet. If you need someone, I can look for a receptionist or an assistant."

He shook his head. "I'm all right for the time being." He wanted to ask about the person she was meeting, if that was the truth, and David wasn't sure it was. He'd been keeping track of the number of miles from where he picked her up. So far they were three miles out. She'd planned to walk this far and farther. Obviously, she didn't have a car. Probably not a cell phone, either.

"It's right over there."

David angled the car into a parking lot and pulled into a space near the door. "What time are you supposed to meet this...person?"

Rose checked the clock on the dashboard. So she also had no watch. Many people checked their cell phones for the time, but it came to mind that he'd never seen her checking or even holding a phone.

"She should be here now," Rose said.

She opened the passenger door. David moved faster and was around the car to hold it for her. He reached into the back and pulled out her briefcase.

"Well, have a good weekend," she said.

"You, too, but before I leave, do you have a ride home?"

She nodded. "My friend will drive me to my door." Her voice stressed the last few words.

The Grogg wasn't a four- or five-star establishment. It was a pub. David smelled the grease in the air, mingled with stale beer. Reluctant to leave her alone, David opened the door of the pub and held it for her.

"You don't have to come in."

"I know. Do you mind if I have one drink? I've had a long week, too."

Defeated, she walked into the darkened building. Inside, the place was loud with Friday evening drinkers. Huge televisions hung from every area of the room, all of them set to sports channels, except for one that offered the news, with closed-captioned words running across the bottom of the screen.

"Hi, Amber," Rose said to a woman behind the counter as she slipped onto a bar stool. David took the stool next to her.

"Hi." Amber held on to the word as if it was the end of a song. Her attention was directed at David. "Who's this?"

"Amber Waverly, meet David Thorn," Rose said.

"Thorn? Of the House of Thorn?"

"Guilty," he said, and smiled.

"Nice to meet you." She dried her hands on a towel, then shook hands with him. "What can I get you?" she asked while she worked on someone else's drink.

"Scotch, straight up," he said.

Nodding, she placed the drink she'd made in front

of Rose. A moment later, a glass was in front of him. David took a sip.

"I'm checking out," Amber said to Rose. "Stay here. I'll be ready in a few minutes." Then she looked at him, a mischievous gleam appearing in her eyes and a sly smile curving her lips. "We're going to dinner. Want to join us?"

David was sure he heard a catch in Rose's throat. He glanced her way, but her expression told him nothing.

"It will be my treat," David said.

Amber grinned and walked away, or he should say she sashayed down the length of the bar and disappeared through a door to a back room. David looked at Rose.

"Cheers," she said, saluting him with her glass, but unlike Amber, there was no mirth in either her eyes or her voice.

David drank and exhaled at the same time. At least, he thought, she wasn't meeting another man.

Chapter 4

Rose's mouth dropped open when she saw Amber striding toward them. She'd changed into a dress. Gone were the jeans and shirt with the Grogg's logo on the pocket she'd been wearing behind the bar. Her hair had been pulled to one side and anchored with a comb. Curls hung loosely from that side and bounced about her face. Their movement reminded Rose of young girls flipping their hair in an attention-getting, look-at-me gesture. Her makeup had also been refreshed to the point that her eyes twinkled with eyeliner and mascara.

Had she done this because of David? Rose's expression hardened as she clamped down on her back teeth.

"Ready?" Amber asked, slipping the strap of her purse over her shoulder.

Amber didn't like eating at the Grogg. It wasn't the

food. Dining there made her feel as if she was always at work. They planned to eat at Kelly's, a place not too far away. Amber knew the chef there. The food was good, the atmosphere welcoming, and they always got pleasant smiles from the staff.

Tonight was no different. As they arrived, Amber was greeted with a smile and a bear hug.

"Apparently, she's known here," David commented.

Rose gave him a look, but said nothing. They were led to their table and handed menus. Rose buried her face in hers, although she knew it practically by heart. At least she knew the dishes she liked best.

When the waiter arrived, David quickly ordered champagne. Rose equated champagne with celebrations like birthdays and anniversaries, not a meal on a Friday after work.

"What should we drink to?" Amber asked, her glass already high in the air.

"How about to new experiences?" David suggested.

Both women looked at him.

"Rose has a new job. I've just moved to the area and the store is a new experience for me," he explained.

"And I've just met you," Amber said, pushing her glass forward.

They clinked and drank.

Soon, their food arrived and conversation was put on hold until everyone was served. Dinner was a total and complete disaster. Rose hadn't had champagne in over a year. She drank one flute, telling herself that would be enough, but as Amber and David traded stories and laughs, Rose traded one drink for multiple refills of the bubbly liquid.

If she was frank with herself, it bothered her that Amber was so friendly with David. They acted as if they'd known each other for years and she felt like the new kid in school that no one talked to. Occasionally, David or Amber would ask her a question, but she felt invisible to the two of them. True, Rose and David hadn't started on the right foot, but she felt they were making progress toward friendship.

Twenty minutes after they'd finished eating, Rose had had enough. Excusing herself to the bathroom, the champagne hit her the moment she stood up. Refusing to raise her hand to her head, she made it to the ladies' room without the dizziness enveloping her or tripping over her own feet. She wanted to leave, but she couldn't just go without a word. Amber would think something terrible had happened to her. It was their history. They looked out for each other. After meeting during the building's collapse in the hurricane and keeping each other alive, both felt responsible for the other.

Rose fumbled through her purse, looking for her cell phone. She hadn't carried it much since the accident. When she'd needed the phone the most, there was no communications available and it was totally submerged in dirty water anyway. Afterward, she no longer looked at it as her lifeline. Having it attached to her hand like an extension of her fingers, the way she had before the storm, was no longer wanted or needed. But right now, she was glad she had it. Her elation turned to sadness when the low-battery light flashed once and went out.

Defeated, her hand dropped to the counter in front of the mirror. She looked down, but not at her reflection. Behind her the door opened and closed.

"Are you all right?" someone asked.

Rose looked up at someone who couldn't be older than the legal drinking age.

"Just a little too much to drink," she said.

"Been there, done that." The young girl smiled sympathetically.

"I want to text my friend, but my phone is dead." She held the useless phone up for the girl to see. "Do you have one I could use?" Rose's speech was slurred. It was difficult to talk. She knew she had to go home. "I need to tell her I'm taking a taxi home."

"Sure." She whipped out her phone and passed it over as if it was the most natural thing to do.

Rose had a hard time remembering what to do. Her brain was foggy. She glanced again at the young girl.

"Give me her number and I'll text her," the girl said.

Passing the phone back, Rose said, "Tell her I'm taking a taxi home."

After putting in the number, the girl typed the message.

"I'll help you to the curb," the girl said, storing her phone in her purse.

"I'll be all right," Rose told her. Somewhere in the depths of her brain, she knew she wanted to leave under her own power. Why was unclear, but she'd survived worse. She could get as far as a taxi without help.

She left the room, looking in the direction of the table where Amber and David were probably laughing at some story one or the other was relating. The table wasn't visible from where Rose stood and she was thankful for that.

Rose headed for the door, watching it closely as it yo-yoed back and forth in a wavering vertigo pattern. Why did she drink all that champagne?

Someone took her arm and held it tightly. She turned, alarmed, pulling away in fear. David was holding her.

"Let me go," she said.

"Another word and I'll carry you out of here," he said. His tone of finality got through to her. The words had a sobering effect.

"Where's Amber?" she mumbled.

"Right here," Amber answered from the other side of her.

Together they led her outside. David released her long enough to open the car door.

"Amber?" she called.

"David offered to take you home," Amber explained. "I'll call you tomorrow."

Rose couldn't refuse to get in the car. She had no control over her muscles. They, along with her speech, seemed to abandon her.

David angled her into the car and she watched as Amber walked to hers. Only after her friend was behind the wheel did David get in.

"I'm sorry," Rose said.

"No apologies," he said shortly.

She said nothing during the quick ride to her apartment building. She concentrated on keeping her eyes open. She'd fallen asleep once in David's car and woken up practically in his arms. Even with her mind muddled, she wasn't going to let that happen again.

"You and Amber seem to have a very special friendship," David said when they'd left the busy traffic area and were entering a residential neighborhood.

"We've known each other awhile." Rose didn't commit to any specifics. Actually, she couldn't. It was hard to get her words out in a coherent order.

Despite her resolve to remain awake, the steady rhythm of the car made her doze off. When she opened her eyes again, they were parked in front of her building. David had turned her legs to the street. He was pulling her out of her seat.

"What are—" She didn't get any further. Her head exploded with pain.

He supported her with his arm around her waist. She stumbled on the first step. David caught her, his arm pulling her tighter against him. Rose was barely awake when they entered her apartment.

He sat her on the sofa. She fell sideways, her arm grazing the floor. "I am so fired," she muttered. "I shouldn't drink…"

Then she felt her legs being lifted. She tried to open her eyes, but it was too much work. She wanted to laugh, yet felt no sound come out. Who had her legs? She giggled as they settled.

"I'm fired, Amber," she said, unaware that Amber wasn't there. "David will fire…" She trailed off.

"Shh."

She heard a sound. Her eyes still wouldn't open. Rose puckered her lips and blew. The noise was awful.

"Go to sleep."

There was that voice again. Who was that? Rose didn't have time to think. Something warm covered her. She shrugged into it and slept.

"Ohhhh," Rose groaned, raising her hand to ward off the sunlight. She hadn't felt this bad since she accepted a Phi Delta fraternity challenge. Determined to not allow any guy to outdrink her, she'd surpassed them all. Standing up as the last one fell, she'd stepped over him and walked back to her dorm, with the help of her roommate. The victory was short-lived. The next morning she could barely open her eyes and her mouth felt like she had a ball of straw in it.

Just like this morning, and she hadn't drank a fraction of what she had then. She had to go to work. The thought stopped her and she sat straight up. She fell off the couch, her bare feet tangled in the afghan. Pain knifed through her head. She realized it was Saturday and the workweek was over. She leaned back against the couch and closed her eyes. It would take too much of an effort to try and climb on it.

Thoughts of the list of things she needed to get done floated on her soaked brain. She'd planned to go in where she'd be alone. David wouldn't be there.

"David," she said. "I was with David."

Her entire body went hot. David had been there when she started drinking and she had a vague memory that he took her home. Rose tried to focus on the memory, but she couldn't pull it in. Amber had been there, hadn't she? Rose wrinkled her nose. Yes, Amber had been there. She'd met Amber for dinner. It stood to reason that Amber would take her home. Pushing herself up, Rose looked at the door. David had been in the apartment before. Yet somewhere in a crevice of her mind she pictured him close to her in this room. Her hand went to her hair. Then her jaw. Had he touched her?

Again, a blast of furnace air hit her. She needed a shower. Rose pushed herself to her feet. She stumbled to the small kitchen and put on some coffee. It seemed to take forever for it to drip into her cup. Taking a cautious drink, she breathed heavily. After a second drink, she took the cup and headed for the shower. There was still work on her schedule.

That is if she still had a job. And she didn't think she did.

Rose showered and dressed, taking care to keep anything from clanging. She got to the office two hours later than she planned. Checking the whiteboard in the outer office, she saw that it had been updated. Today's date had been written on the column labeled Saturday. David's name was checked in and he was apparently in the store somewhere. Rose groaned. She wouldn't go looking for him. Her stomach clenched at the thought of her actions the previous night.

The phone rang, startling her. Quickly, she rushed to her desk and picked it up to stop the ringing.

"House of Thorn," she said. Her voice was lower than its usual pitch.

"How are you?" Amber said.

"Amber?"

"Yes, who'd you think this was? Did you get home all right last night?"

So Amber hadn't taken her home. Rose leaned against the side of the desk, her back to the door. "I suppose. I woke up in my apartment this morning, on the couch, fully dressed except for my shoes."

"And you're proud of that?" Amber laughed.

"Why didn't you take me home?" Rose asked.

"You were well out of it. And if you passed out—"

"I did not pass out," Rose interrupted.

"You could have. And if that happened, I couldn't get you up those stairs. And speaking of stairs. Now that you have a well-paying job, you should think of moving."

Rose hung her head in the hand that wasn't holding the phone. She needed another cup of coffee. There was none in the office, but there was a concession stand in the lobby. There was also construction noise that made her head feel like someone was using a jackhammer inside it.

"Not today," Rose said.

"Are you hungover?"

"Absolutely. I know I drank too much."

"That you did," Amber confirmed. "Why? You never drink a lot."

"Why were you so up in David's face? You were flirting with him."

"Testing him," she amended.

"What does that mean?"

"I wanted to see if he was open to relationships."

"Why?"

Rose heard Amber sigh into the phone. "Because…"
She paused. "I have a friend who's interested in him
and—"

"Stop!" Rose sat up straight. She ignored the pain in
her head, but shut her eyes against the sunlight filtering through the windows.

"Don't deny it. I could see it in the way you looked
at him when you didn't think anyone saw you."

"I didn't look at him any special way." Silence came
from the other end of the line. After a prolonged period
of time, Rose said, "Amber?"

"I'm here."

Rose heard a muffled sound in the background. "But
I have to go. We'll talk about the way you look at him
later tonight."

"I didn't look at him in any special way," she said
as loud as she could, but Amber had already broken
the connection.

Rose replaced the receiver and stood up. David was
standing in the doorway.

Her shoulders dropped. It wasn't even lunchtime yet
and her day was already a fiasco.

"Am I fired?" she asked.

"Why would you think that?"

"Last night…" She didn't finish the sentence.

"You were on your own time. What you do away
from the office is your business."

It was hard to keep standing. She wanted to sit down,
but she didn't want David towering over her, since his
height already made her feel short.

"How do you feel?" he asked.

There were several answers Rose could give David, but she opted for the truth. "Like there are little men in my head with jackhammers."

He stepped into the office. "Drink this."

"What is it?" Rose asked.

"Orange juice with a pain reliever dissolved in it." He pushed the carton toward her. "It'll help your head and the sugar in the juice will cause the alcohol in your system to burn faster."

Rose accepted the carton and used a straw to take a long swallow. After a breath, she continued until she'd gotten to the end of the drink.

"If you want to go home, you should."

Rose shook her head. She'd already gone home once for being tired. She wasn't planning to make a habit of it and she was stronger than alcohol. She would beat this headache and she'd get something done. It might be only one thing, but one was better than none.

"I'll leave you alone then."

Rose stopped him from leaving. He turned back to her.

"You took me home," she stated.

"Amber lived in the other direction," he explained.

"Thank you," she said. "I apologize for drinking—"

He raised his hand, stopping her. "We all do it at one time or another. No apology necessary."

Rose thought of the young girl she'd seen in the ladies room who'd also understood her plight. Yet neither of them understood why Rose drank so much. She had a hard time giving that question an answer, too. And an even harder time wondering about last night and what David had done in her apartment.

"Where are you going now?" Rose asked.

"Back to the store. Is there anything you need?"

"No," she said.

He turned away.

"Yes," Rose said, contradicting herself.

David turned back. She said nothing for a moment. David raised his eyebrows, waiting for her to go on.

"In my apartment last night…" She stopped, unsure how to ask her question.

"Yes," he said.

"Did you touch my hair?" she asked in a rush before she could change her mind.

The atmosphere of the room changed in an instant. David's look almost liquified her. It was hot and sensual. She could feel the heat and electricity in the air between them as surely as she'd feel a shock to her feet.

He took a step toward her, then another. Rose wanted to move, run, back away, but his look riveted her to the floor. Even if she wanted to move, she was incapable of the action.

"Do you mean, did I run my hand down this side?" He demonstrated by touching his palm to the center of her head and smoothing it down her face until he reached her shoulder. "Did I brush my knuckles over the smoothness of your jaw from cheekbone to chin?"

Rose held her breath. She couldn't breathe for the heat that burned through her at his touch.

"Did I lean over you and plant a kiss on your cheek as tender as if you were a child?"

She found her feet then and moved back so he couldn't fulfill that suggestion. Rose didn't remember his lips on her skin. The memory of his hand on her hair and face was as unclear as if she'd seen it in a dream, or behind a gauzy curtain, and was unsure if it really happened.

David dropped his hand and smiled. "No," he said. "You must have dreamed that."

She let out a slow breath. It wanted to whoosh out in one long stream, but only through a Herculean effort did Rose allow it to expel slowly.

"I probably did," she said, unsure if she was apologizing to him for actions she had a hard time remembering.

"Yes," he agreed. "Ever had a hangover before?"

"I went to college," she said by way of explanation. "We had our wine parties."

"But it's been a while since that happened," he stated rather than asked.

"Yes," Rose answered, not wanting to admit exactly how long ago that was.

"It might take some time, but it will wear off."

Rose wanted to get back to work. She wanted something to do other than think about that scene that developed in her mind while David reenacted what may or may not have happened. He was too clear with his description of what she thought had happened. Yet he said she dreamed it.

If so, it was a very real dream. Yet, she was sure he hadn't kissed her. That, her body would remember, even if her mind didn't.

* * *

Rose had closed the blinds. David knew the light hurt her eyes due to the amount of champagne she'd consumed the previous night. He was sorry he ordered it, but it did make her loosen up some. She was embarrassed this morning. Still, he couldn't take his eyes off her. The subdued light turned her into a temptress and he was tempted. She moved slower, sexier, concentrating on her ability to remain balanced. He'd seen women in her condition before, but never had he wanted to comfort them as he wanted to comfort her.

Maybe it was the part of her he knew. She'd survived the storm and she was making an effort to get back on track, even with him, a man she felt took advantage of her former employer. She took initiative and she delivered.

"Is there something else?" she asked.

David nearly missed what she said. He was staring at her.

"I just want to add that I've agreed to a newspaper interview this week. The reporter will be here on Thursday morning."

She smiled quickly as if it hurt her face to move. "A little publicity will be good for the store."

David wasn't sure if that was a compliment or not. "Just in case I'm not here when he arrives, you'll know who he is and why he's here."

She nodded. "I'll find you if that's the case."

She glanced at the door as if she could see the whiteboard in the other room. David left her, going to his own office. Rose was wearing her hangover as well as she could. It had been an interesting night. He still didn't know what to make of it. Her friend Amber had definitely flirted with him, but at the same time, she seemed to be trying to throw him at Rose. Rose was attracted to him. He could tell from the way she looked at him and acted. He'd been around enough women to understand the nuances of feeling when they were offering more than friendship.

He wondered if she knew it yet. Was she fighting it?

David strode to the window and looked out at the building that bore his name. His back stiffened. Maybe Rose did understand. He should remember that affairs with employees more times than not ended badly. He relied on her. She was sharp and she was leading the renovation faster than he could have. He needed her.

It was better for the business and their personal lives if they kept everything between them on a professional basis. David turned back to his desk. He took a seat and reached for his computer keyboard. He looked up as Rose passed by his office door. She stopped a second to write on the whiteboard. David heard the outer door open and close. Turning his attention back to his work, he was distracted by the light scent of Rose's perfume wafting through the air.

Chapter 5

By Thursday Rose was back to normal. She regretted her actions the night David joined her and Amber, and she knew better than to take more than one drink in his presence ever again. It was unlikely that she would break that rule, since in the past few days she'd remembered her policy of staving off any romantic relationships with employees. That went for employers, too. David had hired her to do a job and if she was to be successful, she needed to keep her eye on her goal.

Thorn's was going to be beautiful when it was finished. The renovations were happening faster than expected. She missed Bach's, yet her life had changed, so why shouldn't the store? The architect and builders had things well under control. It was time to start looking at inventory and supplies. For these she was going to need to start hiring soon. The office wasn't large, but with just another assistant around she'd have a buffer between herself and David. And she knew exactly whom to start with.

Rose had just put her hand on the phone when the sound of the office door caught her attention. David was out. Had he returned earlier than he told her he would?

After a moment, when he didn't pass or appear in her doorway, she got up and went to see who was there. Her teeth clenched when she saw the short man standing at the vacant receptionists' counter. The newspaper interview. She'd forgotten it was today. Of all the reporters in Logan Beach, why would Jim South be interested in a piece on a department-store opening? Rose wanted to step back into her office, but it was too late. Jim was already turning toward her. He'd obviously heard her walking to the door.

"Hello," he said with a smile. "I have an appointment with David Thorn."

He hadn't acted like he recognized her. Would she be lucky enough to have him miss who she was?

"He's in the store right now. I'll call him. You can wait over there." Rose indicated a sofa that had been in the room when she came that first day. She didn't wait for the reporter to sit down and she didn't offer him anything to drink. She forced herself to turn and walked calmly to her desk.

David arrived within minutes of her call and the two men left the office so the reporter could tour the building's progress. She took a sigh of relief at their departure. From her experience, reporters liked to take down the facts and leave as quickly as possible. As there wasn't much to see or hear in these offices, Rose felt certain they would not return together. Still, she'd been stressed by his appearance.

Did he remember her? He didn't indicate that he did, but she'd retreated to her office quickly and he'd never seen her looking the way she did today. She was healthy, had gained some of her weight back and no longer looked like a starving refugee. If he'd noticed her, he might want to do a follow-up story. She wouldn't agree to that, but she understood that meant nothing to a reporter of his type. To him the story was everything, regardless of what the victim—and she considered herself a victim—wanted.

It took Rose a while to convince herself that her past was behind her. Jim South had no reason to remember her or that he'd once done a story where she and Amber were the main focus. Two cups of chamomile tea later, she made her first call to hire an assistant. She got no answer and left a message. Twenty minutes after she drained a third cup, two male voices shattered her calm. David was back and Jim South was on his heels.

Rose prayed they'd go to David's office and finish the interview. Luck wasn't with her. They stopped at her door and David introduced her as the only other employee.

"Not for long," she said. "I started the hiring process today."

"Say, aren't you…"

The reporter didn't get to finish his sentence. Rose's

phone rang and she checked the caller ID. "I have to take this," she said, feeling no guilt for the white lie.

David and Jim left her office and she closed her eyes, then took a long breath before picking up the phone.

After a few more questions and several surreptitious glances toward Rose's office, the two men shook hands and David saw Jim South out. David's cell rang before he reached his office. It had rung three times before he answered it.

"How's it going at the beach?"

Immediately, he recognized his brother's voice.

"Blake! What's going on?" He dropped into his chair and swung around to look through the window. A surge of brotherly love went through him. He and Blake had a special relationship. Although David had a special relationship with both of his brothers, it was different with Blake. The two of them seemed to be on the same wavelength.

"I was sitting here in cold San Francisco, thinking of you with warm balmy breezes, a bright sandy beach, and wishing I was there."

"Well, it's your own fault. You chose San Francisco."

"After you snapped up the queen of choices," Blake replied.

David laughed haughtily. "San Francisco isn't that cold."

"Not very, at least not at this moment. But it surely isn't as warm as it is at Logan Beach."

"True," David admitted. The temperature outside was in the high eighties with low humidity. It would be perfect for being outside, but he wasn't outside. He was working.

"So what's happening?" Blake asked. "Did you ever reach that woman about the store?"

David's stomach contracted. "I did."

"And did you convince her to work for you? Or have we found the first woman on the planet to refuse your efforts to gain her attention?"

"I'm not trying to get her attention."

"So she is working for you?"

David walked right into that. Now he had to admit that Rose was at the store. But that's all he'd admit. His attraction to her would remain within his control.

"It appears to be working out with her."

"What does that mean?"

"When I explained that I wanted her to work at the store, she agreed." That was skimming over the truth, but there was no reason for Blake to know the full and complete truth.

"Wow, your powers of persuasion must be equal to your courtroom arguments. A woman who wouldn't even return your calls just came to work for you when you asked."

"What can I say, I'm good," David quipped. "But you didn't call to ask about a woman you've never met. So what's going on?" David redirected the conversation. Discussing Rose was uncomfortable, even with his brother.

At that moment, he heard the outer office door open and close. Rose was back. David saw her pass his door on her way to hers. She looked inside and then continued. His heart beat a little faster and he smelled her perfume. The scent was light, so light he should only be able to distinguish it when he stood close to her, but somehow he'd become aware of her scent.

Blake sighed into the phone. David returned his attention to his brother. He knew Blake was about to ask for a favor.

"I have a favor to ask."

Another one, David thought, but waited for Blake to continue.

"I have a candidate you might be interested in."

"Candidate for what?"

"Personnel director."

No wonder he'd asked about Rose and whether he'd reached her.

"The thing is, I know of a very good personnel director. We were at school together. I ran into him a few days ago and he told me he's looking for a position."

"And you thought of me?"

"Well, you are putting a store together practically from the ground up."

"Send me his information. I'll pass it by Rose."

"Rose?" Blake asked.

"Yes," David said. And left it at that.

David mentioned that the store should keep as many of the personnel from Bach's as they could. In theory that was good, but practice proved a different animal. With the sale negotiations and the renovations taking months, many of the employees had either found jobs or were looking for them.

Rose remembered Melanie Owens, a bright woman in her twenties who'd worked as the Bachs' assistant. Wondering if she was still unemployed, Rose spoke to her and, as luck would have it, Melanie jumped at the chance to return. She had a job that required a long commute. Leaving it wasn't an issue, she'd told Rose. It would allow her to be closer to home. Rose cautioned her that the job would be different from what she'd done before and they should discuss it first.

They agreed to meet for lunch next week. Rose wished it had been today, so she could get out of the office and forget that she'd seen Jim South again. She tried to concentrate after he left, but all she thought of were the glaring newspaper reports of her rescue and her loss. South had used her suffering as silage for his biased accounts of her personal tragedy. Pushing those thoughts aside, she picked up the phone again, but put it back without making a call.

Moments later a former employee named Olivia called to ask for a meeting in the morning, but didn't want to get into details on the phone. Rose added it to her schedule, then she jumped when a knock came on her door. Looking up as David opened it, she concealed her relief that he was alone.

"I don't think I've ever seen this door closed. May I come in?"

"Of course," she said. "I had a call to make and didn't want to disturb you and Mr. South."

"South is gone. We can expect his story in the Sunday edition."

Rose's shoulders dropped in relief and she tried to

cover her discomfort. "That's good timing, since the hiring will begin soon. I have two meetings tomorrow with potential candidates."

David checked his watch. "I have an afternoon meeting, but I could join you in the morning. I'd like to meet some of the candidates."

"All right," she said tentatively.

"I also want to talk to you about something else, but we can do that at our staff meeting."

Their staff meetings consisted of updates on what was going on and what was planned. They were short and focused.

"In the meantime, I haven't yet viewed the site where the major part of the storm struck. Would you go with me?"

Rose's head snapped up. "You want to go there?" She tried to keep her voice normal, but even she could detect it was several notes higher than her usual conversational tone.

"Jim South asked some very interesting questions about the area. You said I should understand what happened and what the people here feel. I thought that would be a good place to start."

Rose didn't say anything, but she wasn't enthusiastic about the trip. Who would be? she asked herself. People lost their possessions and some died, but Rose understood that people who didn't live through it wanted to see what had happened. It was natural for them. She knew that. But for her, she'd be fine living her life never venturing down any of those streets again. However, that was not to be. She realized that David needed to see what a new department store meant to the community.

Rose's throat closed off. After a moment, she said, "Sure. There isn't much to see. The storm was massive as you know. Efforts by FEMA were hampered with red tape and even now, many areas are still waiting for renovation or rebuilding."

"I'm sure they've made some progress in cleaning things up, but I can't tell you how many people mention it first when I tell them I'm setting up a store in Logan Beach."

"When would you like to go?" she asked.

"Now, if it's convenient."

It was never going to be convenient, Rose thought. It was close to the end of the day. She wished they could take separate cars and then go home from there, but suggesting it would appear rude. She wouldn't want to return to the office and David was so perceptive that she didn't want to be confined in a small car with him after viewing the area.

But it seemed as if she had no choice.

"Afterward, we could get something to eat," David said. "We could use the time to have our staff meeting."

He waited for her to answer. Rose took a long time thinking about it. "Give me ten minutes," she said. "I'll meet you in the parking lot."

"See you there," he said.

Rose hadn't waited for him to go to the parking lot together. She walked straight to a late-model compact car. It wasn't new, but it had been recently washed.

There was no dust from the construction going on at Thorn's that seemed to cover everything in this area.

David caught up with her. "I didn't think you had a car," he said. "I saw you get on a bus earlier this week."

"It was being serviced. Get in."

Obviously, she planned to drive. David moved to the passenger side and folded his large frame into the small car.

"This is probably as close as I can get," Rose said several minutes later as she inched the car into a parking space. "We'll have to walk from here."

She opened the door and got out. The ocean air was stronger here and she took in a deep breath. David stood up and looked around as he closed the car door. The area had broken buildings, with caution tape that had been there so long it was torn and flapping in the breeze. Signs saying the places were unsafe were posted on every structure Rose could see.

David took a few steps and Rose joined him. She could hear the echo of her own steps and feel the grit under her shoes, even though the walkways, where they still existed, had been cleared. They walked two blocks, but only she knew that. She knew what used to be in the empty spaces, what the remnants of broken buildings had once housed.

As well as the salt in the air, there was also the lingering odor of debris. Rose coughed as she remembered that smell.

"If this is what it looks like now," David commented as they stopped, his voice low enough that he could have been talking to himself, "it must have been much worse right after the storm subsided."

"It was," Rose said. She wasn't sure if the words had been vocalized or she'd thought them. It was unbelievable the way things looked.

David began walking again. Rose followed but then came to a full stop. She squeezed her eyes shut, clenched her jaw and balled her hands into fists. Memories flooded her mind, coming in waves like the unrelenting ocean in the distance. She tried to force them aside, but they kept coming, returning, taking her back to that wet space under the house, to that small crevice of air and water where she was trapped, immobile until rescue workers found her.

The sun hadn't reached her and even day had felt like night. Then the flash of cameras, the barrage of questions coming at her from all directions. She'd had no bearings as strong arms lifted her onto a stretcher. There was one comforting voice that penetrated the cacophony of sound. Rose reached for it, trying to hear it and focus on it. Everything hurt, every movement of her body, every shift of the stretcher. It hurt to breath after being pinned down so long. Her legs were too numb to feel and her arms were useless.

Now, Rose drew in a long breath and turned toward the sea. Using all the effort she had, she concentrated on the sound. She needed to go somewhere else, even if she couldn't be there physically, she needed to find a mentally safe place. She and Amber had said that to each other when either of them suffered a panic attack.

Rose took another deep breath and imagined the

meadow. She filled in the color of swaying grass and wildflowers. She brought their scent to her mind and felt the breeze kissing her cheeks and playing with her hair. Her body relaxed, and she unclenched her hands. Dragging her fingers, she skimmed the tops of the long-stemmed flowers, allowing their caress to calm her. A distant grassy field beckoned. She went toward it, seeing the colorful greens changing, as if an invisible mower cut irregular curves in the emerald design. She used the technique she and Amber had employed while they'd waited for help to come. It still worked.

Eventually, her face muscles loosened as she took in the virtual scenery. She didn't know how long she stood there. Time had ceased to exist. Her mind had completely closed off reality and she lived in a world of blue skies and exotic scents.

"Rose?"

Roses grew at her feet. Their perfume reminding her of...

"Rose?"

Her eyes flew open at the sound of her name. David stood close enough to kiss. She moved to take a step back, forgetting that the ground was broken and uneven. As she stumbled backward, David's arms, strong and sure, shot out and caught her, pulling her against him.

Emotion overwhelmed Rose and she crumpled against him. She shuddered, but kept herself from crying. She just leaned against him, holding him, taking his strength as her own. His arms surrounded her, hugging her to him and allowing her to stay there until she was able to push herself away.

David said nothing. As she moved back, his arm stayed around her waist. She didn't need the added support, but wanted it. She liked the way he felt and the way she seemed to fit in his arms. He led her away from the site and they walked in silence for a while. When they reached the seawall she leaned against it. David stood quietly next to her. Rose could feel the warmth of his body, but she didn't turn for several moments.

His eyes were steady with concern as he gazed at her. She took a long swallow, followed by a deep breath.

"What happened?" he asked gently. "I saw your reaction when the reporter recognized you. He was about to say something. That's why your door was closed when I came by earlier."

She nodded.

Across from them was a street vendor. Rose moved toward him and his cart. David followed. She ordered two bottles of water and handed one to David. Then she moved to the warm sand and sat facing the blue ocean. Small waves crashed against the shoreline.

"My house was over there," she began. She hooked her thumb over her shoulder, not bothering to look behind her. "On Ocean Avenue. It was built in the 1920s. It had survived war, depression, fire and presidential elections, but the Atlantic proved to have more power than any of the others."

She looked again at the vast ocean. It was calm, showing no indication of the devastation it could unleash on so many lives. Gulls cawed above them, occasionally dipping into the water in search of a meal.

"Once the storm was over everything was gone." Her

voice hitched on the last word. David reached over and took her hand. She took another shuddering breath. "I lost my fiancé and probably would have died, too, had it not been for Amber."

"Amber was there?"

Rose nodded. "We were pinned under the debris. Neither of us could see the other. We'd been knocked out by flying objects. I came to under a collapsed building. I could only move one arm and I was laying…" She stopped as memories of the ordeal leaped into her mind.

"Take your time," David said, his voice quiet and comforting.

She turned her face up to the sun and let the warmth soak into her skin. "I was engaged," she stated. Between them the air stilled. Her hand remained in his. She felt no tightening, no loosening of his grip.

"What happened to him?"

"He died during the storm." Rose paused. She pursed her lips to keep them from trembling. "His name was Greg—Gregory Taylor." She hadn't thought of Greg in weeks, not since she'd begun working at Thorn's.

"Are you all right?" David asked.

She nodded and took a drink from the bottle of water she'd just twisted open.

"What did Greg do?"

"He was an EMS worker." She smiled, remembering. "His dream was to be a doctor and he was working to save money for medical school."

Again, emotion welled up inside her and she swallowed it to keep from succumbing to its will.

"I wasn't there. He rang my cell phone, but I couldn't

reach it. I lay in a few inches of dirty water for three days before rescue came. By then—by then Greg was gone."

"What happened to him?"

"He was trying to help someone, pull a man from the rubble of a destroyed house. The rainwater had dug a trench in the sand and he fell into it." She kept her voice steady and as impersonal as she could, repeating the story she had been told. "A wall on a house nearby collapsed, knocking him out and pinning him under it. When they found him…" Again she stopped, took a long swallow and gathered herself. "Both arms and both legs were broken in several places. He couldn't move." The broken bones weren't what killed Greg. Thoughts of Andy, Greg's partner, telling her that Greg had drowned in three inches of water was something she couldn't repeat.

"Before that," she said on a deep breath, "I'd already lost both my parents—my father had a heart attack a week before the storm and my mom died of cancer several years ago. Our house was a total loss."

"I am so sorry."

"Please, don't say anything," Rose said, stopping him. She'd heard all the words people said before and her emotions were very near the surface right now. She had to control them in front of David. He was still her boss and she wanted him to think of her as competent and efficient, not weak and needy.

"Before the storm hit, why did you stay here? Why didn't you just leave?" David asked.

Rose's stare became a glare. "Leave!" she shouted, pulling her hand free. "Why didn't we *just* leave?"

David flinched at her intensity. He had to know he'd touched a sore spot.

"Don't you think we tried? The roads were clogged. There was no warning that we wouldn't be safe until it was too late. We tried everything to safeguard ourselves, but in the end nothing worked. So we were trapped—like lab rats running around in circles looking for the door out of a maze."

Rose felt the tension coil inside her like a tight spring. She released it with her words.

"Only there was no door," she continued as if she was talking to someone else. "There was only rain and wind and people trying to save themselves. No one expected the storm to be that potent. We'd survived them before."

She turned and looked at him, but it wasn't David she was seeing.

"I lost everything. One moment everything was fine. The next moment the wind ripped the very walls from my life. We were no better than human matchsticks thrown in the air."

She should have died, too. But she'd been spared to see the aftermath of a fractured life.

David let her rant. She didn't know how long he waited and listened to her, but when she finally stopped talking, he said, "I'm sorry you went through that, that you lost loved ones and that your entire world was uprooted."

Rose calmed down. "I'm sorry," she said. "I didn't mean to unleash on you."

"That's all right. I'm sure you needed it." He paused for a moment, then asked, "Are you ready to go back?"

Without comment, she stood up and turned toward the street, hiding her face from his scrutiny. She walked away, and when David caught up with her, Rose abruptly stopped and faced him.

"Thank you," she said.

"I didn't do anything. I feel a little helpless, wishing I *could* do something to take your pain away."

"You listened," she said. "That helped more than you know."

"I take it you don't tell that story often?"

"Only Amber knows. We were both in the hospital when the news about Greg came."

"Thank you for telling me."

David smiled and Rose returned it. She felt as if a huge weight had been lifted from her shoulders. She was glad David was the person to remove it.

Back in her car, David took the wheel and they drove in silence, not one that was hostile or uncomfortable, but friendly. David didn't return to the office, but drove to her apartment.

"What are we doing here?" she asked.

"It's the end of the day. There was no need to return to the office until tomorrow."

"But my car?"

"I'll drive home and pick you up in the morning."

Rose wanted to protest, but for some reason she didn't. The thought of him picking her up made her heart beat a little faster.

He got out, coming around the hood to open her door.

He took her hand and the warmth Rose felt reminded her of something she thought had died.

David saw her to her apartment door.

"Well," she said awkwardly, "I'll see you in the morning."

Neither of them moved. Rose looked up. For a long moment, she felt as if she couldn't breathe. Something hung in the air between them. She was unsure if it was good or not.

Then David leaned down. Rose held her breath. He put his cheek on hers. He didn't kiss her, didn't move his head so his lips brushed her skin or his mouth skimmed hers—it was only the touching of two faces.

Rose's eyes closed as emotion filled her and threatened to overflow. David was warm and she felt the stirring of arousal. She should push back, but she didn't want to. She wanted to hold him for just a moment longer, then she'd step inside her apartment and say good-night. But she didn't do that. Her arms moved up David's and wrapped around his neck. Her mouth moved toward his at the same time his moved to hers. Rose turned in his arms, feeling the full length of him. It reminded her how long it had been since anyone held her.

David's mouth captured hers, but not in a harsh way. He was tender, skimming her lips in a swaying motion. It made her legs unstable, as if she was at sea, unaccustomed to the movement of water beneath her.

Rose opened her mouth, allowing David access to not only the taste of her, but also her inner soul. She spoke without words, using her body, her hands, the movement of her thighs to speak a language only the two of them would know or understand.

David held back. She knew he wanted to let go of the strength that could subdue her. She wanted him to. She'd wanted it since she'd opened the door of her apartment and saw him standing there. Rose raised her leg, rubbing it up and down his. The action was a catalyst. David pushed her backward into the room. His foot must have clicked the door closed. It was the last sound she heard before he deepened the kiss.

David knew better than to let this get any further out of hand, but he was lost to stop it. Rose had touched him, touched the inside of him, and he would not let her go.

Not yet.

David wanted to know her better. He wanted to know everything about her. His mouth moved to her neck, where he tasted the skin that held that light scent she left in the office air. He could feel her heartbeat, rapid and excited. He trembled at the feel of her pulse against his tongue.

Softly she moaned. The sound gave him encouragement. In the back of his head was a logical stranger, telling him to stop. He ignored the voice. He couldn't stop with Rose. They were on a collision course and there was no way he could derail it.

He kissed her earlobe, ran his tongue over the curved surface, listened to her panting breath as need filled him. Working his way to her cheek, his erection pressed into her. He wanted her more than he could remember ever wanting anyone. Every part of him screamed for him to pull her away from the wall and take her to the bedroom. He could imagine her lying on a soft mattress, his body above hers, as he drove into her until climax released all the emotion that had built up since their initial meeting.

Rose gave as she took. She was passionate and sexually aggressive. She wanted him as much as he wanted her. He ran his hands over her back and bottom, down as far as he could reach before reversing direction and following a slow path back to her waist.

David was close to going over the edge, when that voice in his head got louder. He slid his mouth free of hers, but held her prisoner against the wall. He couldn't go on, no matter how much he wanted to. Rose was too vulnerable. She'd gone through a lot today and making love with someone who knew better than to get involved with an employee was beyond the rules. She didn't feel like an employee as she was pressed against him. Her breathing was returning to normal, yet it was taking longer for his body to return to an unaroused state.

Then Rose began to slide. The two of them reached the floor, their arms entwined. They said nothing. David wondered what she was thinking, but he didn't want to break the mood. He wanted to hold her for now. Her head sat on his shoulder and he kissed the top of her head. After a moment, he looked around the room.

It was full of boxes. Everything had been packed. The windowsills were bare of any adornments. There had only been dying plants when he'd been there before, but even they were gone. The curtains had been removed and only bare light came into the room. He looked down at Rose.

Her arms were still around him, but she'd fallen into a contented sleep. For her it had been an awful day. She deserved some rest. He cradled her closer and looked through the windows at the setting sun.

Chapter 6

For the second time in her life, Rose woke without memory of getting into bed. She was still wearing the suit she'd worn the day before. It was tight and twisted as she tried to loosen the covers.

David! she thought, forcing the bedcovers aside and swinging her feet to the floor. He was supposed to pick her up for work this morning. Pushing the hair out of her eyes, she wondered when he'd left. Then the memory of his kiss came back to her. Her hand went to her lips as if she could capture the fleeting memory and hold it.

She stood up, checking the clock. As she registered the time, she also smelled coffee. She didn't remember setting the coffeemaker to automatically turn on. Padding barefoot to the bedroom door, she pushed it slightly open. She saw nothing. The room looked exactly as it should. She opened the door wider, the smell of coffee stronger. Was David still here?

Rose tiptoed as if she was the interloper. David was in the kitchen, his back to her.

"David, you're still here." The statement seemed sophomoric as soon as she said it. He was standing there beating eggs in a small bowl. A frying pan was on the burner and two slices of bread sat ready in the toaster. "And you cook."

"It was hard," he said. "You have so little food, but I guess that's because you're moving."

Rose glanced over her shoulder at the boxes that littered the room. "I am," she said. "But why are you here?"

Turning around, he poured the eggs into the pan and began to scramble them. "By the time I got up off the floor and carried you to bed, it seemed silly to go home only to come back."

Rose remembered sliding to the floor. She also remembered the prelude that had landed her there—David's kiss. She'd wanted it to be more than a kiss, but he proved to have more sanity than she did. It occurred to her that she hadn't said anything in a while. David finished the eggs and turned them onto a plate. Had he seen her face and understood what she was thinking? Was he thinking the same thing? It wasn't only her face that burned with memory of being in David's arms, but her entire body also got in on the heat transfer.

"David, we don't have time for breakfast." Rose checked her new watch, which had not been removed from her wrist the night before. "We should have been at the office twenty minutes ago. And I have a morning meeting."

"We'll get there. You can drive me to pick up my car and I'll go home and change." He was very calm while Rose seemed to be panicking. She didn't know why. She had a phone number for Olivia. She could call and let her know she was running late.

She'd only vowed a day ago to not compromise her relationship with David and last night she'd forgotten that pledge altogether.

"Why don't you go shower and change. I'll have these eggs and make you some when you come out. Then we can go."

Rose didn't move. She wanted to, but her feet seemed rooted.

"Go," David said, shooing her away.

The gesture released her and she rushed to complete her morning ritual in record time. Ten minutes later she was showered and dressed in a light blue summer suit. Her makeup was minimal and she'd left her hair hanging past her shoulders. Usually, she pinned it up, but today she was not following protocol. Had she followed it since she met him?

"Your breakfast is ready," David called from the other room.

Rose slipped her feet into her heels and then went into the kitchen.

"Wow," David said. "This is what you look like in the morning."

"As do you," she returned. Rose was meeting a potential employee this morning. She hadn't planned what to wear and with only a few minutes to dress, she chose the first thing she could get her hands on that wasn't already packed. Thinking about it after David's comment, Rose saw she was a little more dressed up than usual. With the dust from the construction going on next to the offices they were renting, she often wore clothes that were easy to clean.

David came forward and kissed her on the mouth. Rose tasted coffee and the essence that was him. She felt the kiss all the way to her toes. David held her in a loose hug and kissed her soundly. She wanted it to go on, but David ended the kiss, put his arm around her shoulders and led her to the table.

"Sit here." He pulled out a chair and Rose took a seat.

"I'm not used to having more than coffee and yogurt as I rush out the door. This is wonderful." She took a bite of the omelet he'd prepared, wondering where the green peppers and cheese had come from, but refused to ask.

"Today is a new day," David said, taking the seat across from her and sipping from a glass of orange juice.

"New how?" She was afraid of the answer, but there was no way she could leave that comment hanging.

"The store is almost ready for opening. We, and by we I mean you, can slack off a little. You've been working night and day and I appreciate the effort, but I think it's time for a little R and R."

"Not yet," she said, buttering her toast. "We can celebrate after the official opening, when the shelves are stocked, the employees ready and the departments packed with shoppers."

"It will happen," he assured her. "Are you moving, by the way?" David changed the subject as he glanced at the packed boxes strewn about.

"I found a better apartment closer to the office," she said. "It's also in a safer neighborhood." Amber had been after her for a while to move, but she knew most of the people around here and felt safe with them. With a steady job and an ample paycheck, she felt confident enough to move to better surroundings. Plus she wanted to let the past go. The apartment reminded her of her losses, and after being in David's presence, she knew that a future was possible.

Rose checked her watch again. "I have got to go," she said. Taking a final gulp from her coffee cup, she stood up. As she dumped her dishes in the sink, David came up behind her. He put down his dishes then turned her into his arms for another mind-blowing kiss.

When David returned to the office after Rose left him in the parking lot, he looked as if he'd had hours to groom himself. He wore a gray suit with a blue shirt and dark striped tie. She would swear it had been made for his body alone. Heat poured into her ears as she realized she knew that body better today than she had yesterday. And she wanted to explore it again.

Now!

She took a long breath and let it out slowly. Rose fought to get her emotions in order. Soon they wouldn't be the only people in the office. She wasn't sure about where the change that had occurred last night was going. Neither of them had discussed it.

"Are you ready now?" he asked.

"I'll get my jacket."

Despite Logan Beach being more relaxed than the formal halls of a New York law firm, David still dressed in his lawyer attire. Often he shed the jacket and rolled up his sleeves, but when a meeting was called, he'd go back to being the legal eagle.

On the street, they turned left and Rose saw Olivia Crabtree coming toward them. She wasn't alone. To Rose's surprise, Garth Bonneville and Mary Watley were with her. All three had worked at Bach's.

"Rose, how great to see you," Olivia said, giving her a bear hug. The woman was more friendly than she'd ever been when they saw each other daily.

"It's good to see you all again." Each of them opened their arms, giving Rose no choice but to hug them.

Standing back, she introduced David. Apparent surprise registered on the faces of all three people. "David will be joining us."

Rose felt a current of electricity pass through the group. Then Olivia said, "I thought we might go to Greenstreet for a cup of coffee. It's not that far away."

Rose nodded and the group turned and walked in the direction the trio had come from. She wondered what they wanted…maybe their jobs back. Olivia looked the same as she had before the storm. She'd missed the storm, since she was on vacation, visiting a friend, the week before it hit. Mary and Garth both looked a little weary. Each of them had gained weight, but not enough to warrant a new wardrobe. All three still wore clothing they'd purchased at Bach's.

"Where did you work in the store?" David asked when they'd all gotten coffee and were seated at a table in the center of the room.

"I was in Shipping and Receiving. Mostly on the shipping side," Olivia said.

"I was opposite, on the receiving end," Garth answered.

Mary sipped her coffee. "And I worked in Accounts."

Rose noticed David's head bobbing as he acknowledged each of them.

"So what have you three been doing since Bach's sold?" Rose asked. She was thankful they had survived, but she hadn't seen any of them since the store was sold. Olivia's phone call seemed timely. There was no announcement that Thorn's was hiring yet, so she wondered how Olivia could have tuned in to the store's needs. Or even if she had.

"I've been working for my brother-in-law," Garth said. "He owns a salvage company in Philly."

"Long commute?" David said.

Garth nodded.

"I'm cashiering in a grocery store," Mary said.

"We heard you were back…" Olivia said, then stopped herself. "I mean, we heard you were working at the new store."

Rose nodded. "David asked me to return as assistant manager."

"We wanted to meet you so we could ask for our jobs back."

"We haven't begun the hiring process yet," David said before Rose could answer.

"Do you know when you will?" Garth asked.

"David and I haven't discussed it. We need to fine-tune the details," Rose went on. "However, the Bachs asked that we keep as many employees as possible."

The trio smiled.

"I'm making no commitment," Rose cautioned them. "Thorn's is not the same store as Bach's."

"It'll still have a shipping-and-receiving department," Olivia said.

"And accounting," Mary chimed in. "Someone's got to do it and who better than us. We already know the ropes."

"Not necessarily," David said.

"If not, we're fast learners," Mary said.

"I still have your contact information if it hasn't changed." Rose paused to check their responses. Each nodded. "We're still looking for a personnel manager. When we begin hiring, which will be soon, I'm sure we'll get in touch with you."

Moments later the three left and only Rose and David remained. He got fresh cups of coffee for them and returned to his seat.

"What do you think that was all about?" he asked.

"I'm not sure, but I have a feeling it would have gone differently if you hadn't come along." She gave him a pointed look before sipping the hot drink.

"I agree. They wanted something and didn't want me to know about it." David looked toward the door where the three had left. "How was their work at Bach's?"

"I wasn't in Personnel. No reports about them positive or negative reached me, so I assume they did their jobs satisfactorily."

"Personnel, that's what I want to talk to you about."

Rose wondered where this was going. "I'm meeting a candidate today who I want to be my assistant. She was the Bachs' assistant and she was very good. I want her to be more of a backup assistant manager than a secretary."

"You've worked with her before?"

"She was the Bachs' assistant, but she did so much more than answer phones and keep schedules."

David nodded. "Sounds good."

"But…?" she prompted.

"But we need a lot of employees." He finished the thought she was about to voice.

"I've already contacted a few agencies that I can work with to begin the process."

"I have another plan I want to run by you."

"Go on," she said, apprehensively.

"I spoke with one of my brothers and he has a qualified personnel manager he wants to suggest for the job."

Rose liked the idea immediately. Having someone else take care of that detail was a relief. She saw that she and David worked well together. She almost reached across and took his hand.

"Who is it?" she asked instead.

"I thought I'd put the two of you together and you can iron out what needs to be done."

Rose smiled.

"I'll send you the details. If you want to talk to Blake, I can put you in touch with him."

"Blake? Is that his name?"

David shifted in his seat. He leaned closer to her. Rose forced herself not to do the same. She wanted to touch him, wanted to feel the strength of his hands. They should be talking about the store. It was the only common ground they had. Nothing else could come of their relationship. There was no relationship and could not be one. But her dream came back. The night she drank too much. The night he took her home and put her to bed. He said she'd dreamed of him touching her, but in a manner that she didn't believe.

"Blake is my brother. He runs the San Francisco store."

"And André? He's at the New York store?" she questioned, hoping her memory was correct.

David nodded. "And speaking of stores, we should be getting back," David said.

Rose gathered herself, picking up her purse and sliding off the chair. David gestured for her to pass him. Her arm brushed his as she went by. She stopped and looked at it as if it was no longer attached to her body. Then she looked up at David. They said nothing, but their eyes spoke. Desire was evident in his. Rose couldn't deny that she had the same feelings.

Behind them cups clinked on the counter. The sound broke the invisible cord that held their gazes. David went to the door and held it for her. Rose swallowed the dryness in her throat and followed.

Chapter 7

Grateful for work, Rose was swamped with details—they kept her mind off David. And the addition of Melanie Owens to the staff gave her a needed distraction.

Melanie arrived early on her first day. Rose had come in early, too, trying to get some things settled because she knew Melanie would require a lot of attention the first few days.

"Until we move to the store, this is your office," Rose told her. She showed her around the small receptionist area. "Thorn's is a hard-hat place at the moment." Rose pointed to the white hat on the desk. "We'll go over later so you can see how things are progressing."

Melanie looked around, her face contorted in a small frown.

"What's wrong?" Rose asked.

"Nothing."

Rose knew that wasn't the truth. She spoke the word as if it had the opposite meaning.

"I mean, I thought…"

"I know," Rose said. "It's not the same, but then there have been a lot of changes in our lives and we have to adapt." Rose could practically hear David's voice in her head. They weren't his words, but they had his meaning.

"When do we move to the store?"

"I'd say a week at the most. We'll go over this afternoon and you can see how the construction is coming along. One thing you can do over there is organize your own area. When we get to furniture deliveries you can set it up the way you want it."

Melanie smiled at that. "I always wanted to change the configuration of my setup at Bach's." Melanie turned around in the space. Rose followed her movement. David came toward them.

"David's here. I'll introduce you."

After the preliminaries, the two shook hands and Rose couldn't help thinking about the way he'd looked at Amber. She saw that same look when he smiled at Melanie.

Inside, she felt a twinge of… Rose stopped. What was she thinking? She almost thought jealousy. She couldn't be jealous of Melanie and David. Like she couldn't be jealous of Amber and David. Yet there was a constriction in her chest that was an indication of something she refused to name.

"Welcome, Melanie, glad you decided to rejoin us,"

David was saying when Rose tuned back into the conversation.

The smile the younger woman gave him was bright enough to light the room, but the bulb in Rose dimmed.

"He's much better-looking than his pictures," Melanie commented when David headed back into his office, obvious admiration in her voice.

"Is he going to be a problem?" Rose asked.

Melanie's eyes snapped to hers. "What do you mean?"

"If David's physical attractiveness is going to get in the way—"

"I'm sure it won't," Melanie said quickly.

"Well, then. Let's go tour the store."

Rose smiled, but she was apprehensive. And she shouldn't be. She wanted Melanie in the office to take some of the responsibility off her shoulders, but also to keep Rose...what? Rose paused. To keep her from showing her attractiveness to the man in the other office? But now that it was a fact, Rose realized there were other emotions that came into play and she had not thought them out. After her night with David, she needed to evaluate where that was going, if there was anywhere it could or should go.

What was wrong with him? David asked himself the next morning. He'd asked this same question every morning since he'd first seen Rose. He couldn't go on like this. They couldn't go on like this.

David glared at himself in the mirror as he shaved. The Bachs gave her the highest recommendation and

David could only agree with them. She was an asset to the store, filling in where needed, developing efficiencies and interacting positively with everyone. David couldn't ask for a better assistant manager.

His problem was he wasn't just attracted to her brain or her work ethic. He knew what it was to have an office romance. He'd experienced it firsthand while he worked at the DA's office right after law school. It ruined everything when it fizzled.

When it happened to David, he left the DA's office and joined a firm. It was time for him to move on and the relationship proved the catalyst he needed at the time. Since then, he'd steered clear of women in the workplace.

There were only the three of them in Thorn's temporary offices, but he worked most closely with Rose. He couldn't spend all his time in the store. Even there he thought of Rose. But worse, he wanted to kiss her again. After taking her home from their tour of the devastation site, he'd wanted to keep her in his arms long after it was necessary.

And holding her wasn't all he wanted to do.

He could have returned to his apartment once he'd gotten her settled in her bed, but he didn't want to leave her. Not even when he'd run out to the local deli and grabbed some food. He'd come back and checked that she was still asleep, still waiting for him.

It had taken all his resolve not to crawl into bed with her. He had to make a decision. They'd already crossed a line and it was hard to uncross it without hard feelings. He needed time to think about it and with Rose around that was hard. Whenever he saw her, he wanted nothing more than to rip off her clothes and take her on the floor.

Rose wasn't in the office when he arrived. Melanie, the new assistant, had arrived and was settling in. They greeted each other and David went into his office. He didn't immediately sit down and begin to work. His thoughts were still on Rose.

Standing in front of the window, he looked down on the building next door, wondering where exactly Rose was.

"David." Her voice came from behind him.

He straightened his shoulders and spun around, expecting that she could hear his thoughts.

"We never had our staff meeting. Do you want to do it now?"

David cleared his throat. "Yes, we do have some things to discuss." Most of what he wanted to talk about had nothing to do with the House of Thorn, but Rose always had an electronic notebook full of status reports and to-do lists.

"Shall I invite Melanie to join us?"

"Not this time. Do you mind if we go for a walk instead of using my office?"

She looked confused. This was a departure from their usual arrangement. But Rose agreed and the two of them left the building. They walked toward the ocean. It was a distance away, but not too far on a nice day and today was a nice day. Rose had changed from her heels to the flat shoes she often wore when visiting the store. David remembered walking like this with Blake right after he'd moved to Logan Beach.

"When are you moving?" David asked.

"This Saturday."

"Do you need any help?" He wanted her to say yes. He wanted to see her every day. Moving would mean she wasn't going to be in the office this weekend.

"Amber is coming by, but I've hired a moving company. I don't have that much to move. Most of the stuff in my current apartment came with it. Only a few of the furnishings are mine. So most of the things I'll be leaving behind. The new place will be getting new furniture. I think we'll be fine with my personal items."

Did that mean she didn't want him around? Had her emotions been pulled back in place after the visit to the storm site and she no longer wanted to be near him?

"I met with the personnel director your brother suggested. His name is Carlton Russ—he prefers to be called Carl. He has a lot of experience and will be starting in a week. I offered him the usual package, moving expenses and all."

"Fine," David said. "If he's all right with you, it's all right with me."

David didn't want to talk business. Even though this was a staff meeting, he wanted to talk about her. He had to put the brakes on this. He was moving too fast, not thinking through his arguments.

"He'll begin the hiring process immediately," Rose said.

"Good. I want you to go to New York." He blurted it out, not really thinking about how it would sound.

"New York?"

"It's time we ordered inventory. You were a buyer for Bach's once and gave me a proposal for purchases we should consider."

"I can place that order by phone or using the internet," she said. "I've already ordered some items, the display cases, floor racks and—"

"We need more than that," he interrupted. "This store will have many of the same products all the Thorn's stores have, but since we are located near the shore, we should have some special pieces that reflect beach life."

"You're thinking of unique pieces, not something you can buy in a souvenir shop along the coastline."

"Exactly," he said. "It's amazing how you're always on the same wavelength as I am."

Her head turned and she looked him straight in the eyes. David suddenly understood the double meaning in his words.

"When would you like me to go?"

David wondered if there was also a second meaning in her question.

"I was thinking next week. You already have Melanie working. She seems to catch on very quickly. And we'll be moving our offices into the store as soon as you return. I don't want to interfere with you settling into a new apartment."

"That won't be a problem. I'm sure I can get everything done in time."

Somehow, the two of them had become very formal. David didn't know what he'd said or done to change the casual air that had developed between them. He should let it go. They needed time and space between them. New York would provide that, so why did he want to get closer to her?

"Are you all right?" he asked.

She smiled, but it looked strained. "I'm fine."

"Then why are you speaking so formally? I thought we'd become friends."

"We are friends."

David looked directly at her. He stepped closer and heard her draw in a breath. His hand went to her hair. It was down about her shoulders and felt soft to the touch.

"I want to be more than friends," he said. The words were out before he could stop them. It was as if something inside him overrode his conscious mind. He'd just decided to put some space between them, and here he was stepping closer to her.

He bent to kiss her.

"David, we're on a public street." Rose pushed at his chest.

He looked around. "Yes, we are." His hand curled around her neck and he pulled her mouth to a breath away from his. "If you don't want this, tell me now."

She said nothing, only leaned into him, removing the space and pressing her mouth to his. David cared nothing for where they stood or who watched. He pulled her to him and devoured her mouth with his kisses. He wanted to imprint her with his kiss. David had been with many women, but he'd never wanted one as much as he wanted Rose.

What was it about her that caused the fire in him to burn so hotly? It could flash in a moment, even at the thought of her, or it could start as a slow burn and burst into a conflagration that was hard to control.

Rose pushed back. "We should go back to the office."

"No," he said. "Not today. Let's go to the beach."

"What? We're not dressed for the beach. We have work in the office."

"And it'll be there tomorrow. Let's do it."

Rose took a moment to think about it. "I'll call—"

"No calls," David said, removing the phone from her hand. "We're going to go to the beach and sit in the sand."

"Then what?" she asked.

"We'll decide that when we need to."

She smiled at him and he offered his hand, the one without the phone. Together they ran toward the water.

They came out of the water laughing and splashing each other. Rose hadn't had so much fun in years. They ran toward their blanket and flopped down on it.

"This was such a good idea, we should have done it before." Rose was out of breath. Her words needed an intake of air between each one.

"I would have but I have this assistant manager who's all business. She never takes a break."

She looked around. "Where did all this stuff come from?" Other than the blanket, there was an ice chest, a beach umbrella stuck in the sand, two chairs, a basket with sunscreen, towels, various lotions and a bud vase with three roses in it.

"The same place you got that bathing suit." They'd bought swim clothes at one of the shops along the water.

"That shop didn't sell these things."

"No, it was the one next door. I ordered them while you were deciding between the yellow suit and the black one."

He looked at her, his eyes scanning over her entire frame. She felt as hot as the sun, as if his hands had skimmed over her instead of his eyes. She'd chosen the yellow one. It contrasted with her skin and didn't make her look as thin as the black one did.

"You swim very well," he said.

He pushed a wet tendril of hair to the side of her face. Rose bit the side of her tongue to keep from exhaling in pleasure.

"You forget I've lived here all my life. I used to spend a lot of time on this beach." Rose reached for the cooler to see what was inside—there were fruit cups, yogurt, sandwiches and salads. David had ordered a variety of items. She took a fruit cup and offered him one.

"Used to?"

"There was the storm." She turned and sat in the chair, extending her legs into the hot sand. "It took me six months not to think of the ocean as deadly."

"It must have been awful," David said.

"It was, but let's not talk about it now. The day is beautiful and we're playing hooky from work."

He nodded, taking the chair next to her.

"You swim well, too," Rose said.

"I used to spend a lot of summers on this beach. I kept my swimming shorts and a change of clothes in my car for impromptu beach days."

"Were you a Boy Scout, always being prepared?"

He gave her a deep belly laugh. "Guilty. What about you? Were you dressed in green and gathering badges for good deeds?"

She shook her head. "I was a debutante—white gown, big party, guys who had to be forced to dance with you."

He grinned. "I can't believe that. Who wouldn't want to dance with someone as beautiful as you?"

Beautiful.

The word caught her off guard. Did he think she was beautiful? He was wrong. She wasn't beautiful. Her body was too angular, her neck too long, her hips too broad. Her best features were her long legs and the massive amount of hair that curled and did what she asked of it.

"Aaron Milsap," she answered.

"Who's Aaron Milsap?"

"My date to the cotillion. He ran out on me." Rose laughed. At the time she was both devastated and relieved. Her parents had arranged the date with their best friends. Rose and Aaron disliked each other on sight.

"Where did he go?"

"Off with a cheerleader…a male cheerleader." She frowned.

"And where is Mr. Milsap now?"

"Doctor, not Mister. Last I heard he was in Nebraska…and gay."

"What did you do?"

"I called my father, tried to sneak away so no one knew I'd been jilted and vowed to never, ever go on another blind date."

David laughed.

"Stop laughing," she said, but Rose got the giggles and started laughing, too. "This is not funny, at least it wasn't then. I was devastated. It took a while for me to realize it wasn't him. We both disliked each other and he left to save us further embarrassment."

Her words had both of them howling. Rose felt good. It had been a long time since she'd laughed. She would never have thought to go to the beach during the middle of a workday. She also no longer looked at that huge expanse of water and remembered the wall rising up and thundering down on any and all who got in its path. She'd barely escaped it as she stumbled over trees and bushes trying to find high ground in a place at sea level.

But she'd conquered that fear. David had forced her to face a lot more of her fears. Even though he didn't know it, she was grateful for it.

Turning to look at him, she noticed that he sobered and was looking seriously at the water. She could tell he didn't see it, that his mind was miles away.

"David, is something wrong? You look so serious."

"Nothing's wrong. I was just remembering something."

"What is it?"

"I've been to the legal-aid office a couple of times. They're extremely shorthanded. I helped out for a couple of hours each visit."

"Can you do that? I mean, don't you have to have a license to practice in this state?"

"I do," he said. "I'm licensed to practice in New York, New Jersey and Connecticut."

"You're thinking of volunteering more of your time at the law center?" Rose asked.

"You have everything under control at the store. If you think I need to be there, I'll be there. But if you can handle it, I'd like to volunteer a couple of days a week."

"You don't need my permission for that. You're the manager."

"I know. The store is a big project. There are hundreds of details that need checking and rechecking, not to mention the daily emergencies that crop up out of nowhere."

"I've been handling them," she said. Rose was a little stiff. She wondered if David didn't think she was doing a good job.

"Your work has been excellent," he corrected her thoughts. "I don't know how I would have coped if you'd refused to return."

Rose was suddenly thrown back to that day she found him outside her door. That woman no longer existed. She'd been replaced by someone new, someone better, with a better attitude and a better outlook on life.

Rose turned to fully face David. She'd taken his hands in hers before she thought about what she was doing.

"You're very passionate about helping people," she told him. "I admire that in you. If you think you should do this, then you should."

"You won't think I'm dumping everything on your shoulders? You'll tell me if my being away becomes a hardship for the store. If there is a problem with the opening or any aspect of our schedule."

"I promise," Rose said. The breeze picked up and tiny grains of sand batted against her face and arms. "Today was relaxing, but I suppose there will be no more beach days."

David took her hand. "There will always be beach days."

She glanced at the water, needing to shade her eyes from the glare of the sun reflecting there, but she didn't. She was holding David's hands and reluctant to break contact.

Rose promised herself she'd hold him to the promise of more days like this. It had been wonderful sitting on the sand with him. She'd forgotten about the House of Thorn. She was just a woman on the beach with a man she was extremely attracted to. And he'd gone to a lot of trouble to make her feel comfortable. The food, sunscreen, his concern that he might be adding to her workload.

She could handle the work alone, but she'd gotten used to him being in the office every day. Rose looked forward to seeing him every morning. Now she'd have to be content with three days a week.

But David was passionate about the law. She understood passion. He felt about the law the way she felt about the store. It was a love as strong and needy as breathing. And she would get used to the arrangement. She'd gotten used to not thinking of Thorn's as Bach's. She'd gotten used to not hating David for taking over the former store.

She could definitely get used to only seeing him three days a week. And maybe that would be better for them both. She was attracted to him and hiding it. For two days she wouldn't have to watch what she said and did.

Why didn't that make her feel better?

Chapter 8

Rose was up early taking care of the last few details before the moving van arrived. Everything looked in order. With the curtains gone and the boxes stacked, the room appeared a little brighter. She would not miss this place. It was good to look to the future, especially since she felt it was a bright one.

She was happier than she ever thought she'd be after the storm and after learning of Greg's death. Then Bach's was sold and David came into her life. When the moving van left her today, she'd begin the next segment of her future.

"I'm here."

Rose heard Amber's voice as she shouted from the doorway.

"And look who I found on the doorstep?"

Rose turned. Amber and David stood in the doorway.

"I'm here to help and I brought coffee." He held up a cardboard tray bearing three cups with the logo of a popular coffee house.

"Thanks," Amber said, reaching for one. "I've only had one this morning."

He handed Rose a cup. She noticed her name was printed on the side. "I brought a variety of sweeteners and creamers, since I didn't know how you liked it." He looked at Amber.

"Sweet," she said, taking a couple of sugar packets.

"Okay, just tell me what to do, Rose," David volunteered. "I can carry boxes, stack books, anything you want."

Including cooking breakfast, Rose thought. David had ditched the suit and tie for khaki shorts and a Ralph Lauren T-shirt. The Logan Beach logo had been stitched on the left side. It stretched across his shoulders and chest, defining the strong body underneath, a body Rose had run her fingers over. The shorts bore the same logo. Her face threatened to overheat. She camouflaged it by looking at Amber and smiling. As usual her friend was dressed in loud yellow shorts and and a pink neon shirt; even her matching tennis shoes were bright enough to make you blink in the morning light.

"Where did you get those?" Rose asked.

"I found them in an outlet store. Do you want me to get you a pair?" Amber asked, displaying one foot by shifting her weight and resting her foot on its heel.

"I think I have enough tennis shoes for the time being," Rose answered.

David looked out the window. "I think the moving van is here."

Rose gave David and Amber directions as to what needed to go in the van and what items she planned to take in her car. Two strong men who looked like body-builders arrived, and they quickly began packing the van. Amber cleared the last of the food from the kitchen while Rose made sure the dishwasher was empty.

David helped the two guys, then moved her personal items, computer, dishes, lamps and one live plant to her car.

"So, are you two a couple yet?" Amber asked, when David was out of the apartment and they were working in the kitchen.

"What?"

Amber mimicked the look on Rose's face. "Don't give me that *what?* He wouldn't be here unless there was something going on. I don't remember you telling me you invited him. And from the surprised look on your face when he came in the room, I'd bet good money you were not expecting him."

"I didn't invite him," Rose said. "I didn't even tell him what time I expected the movers to arrive."

"So, I repeat my question. Are you two a couple yet?"

Rose shook her head. "Why would you think that?" The truth was Rose didn't quite have a definition of a *couple*. She and David had shared two kisses, one of them hot enough to melt lead, but that was it. They had no understanding, no discussion of a relationship. David had said a few things that rattled her nerves, but there was no definite togetherness about their association.

Amber reached forward and turned the cup in Rose's hand. "He didn't have to ask how you liked your coffee. And you drank it without even thinking it might be missing the cream and one Equal packet."

"We work in the same office. Obviously, he's seen me make a cup of coffee," Rose argued.

Amber exhaled a long breath, then pursed her lips and let them relax into a mischievous smile.

"I'm sure David is observant. Are you fighting it?" Amber's question arrested her previous explanation.

"Fighting what?"

"An attraction, the need for a man, someone to love, to rely on, someone who's there for you." Amber gave her reason after reason. "I know what happened when Greg died. You retreated into yourself. David is the first man you've let get close to you since then."

"I'm not deliberately avoiding relationships."

Amber gave her the stare. For several seconds she glared at her friend with all-seeing eyes. "Didn't we agree that we wouldn't allow the storm to define us? That we would go forward with our lives? We wouldn't be the broken people we saw happening to others?"

Rose nodded.

"Well, you've been closed in this apartment for two years and now you're making a change for the better. What about a love life? It's not taboo."

"I know." Rose lifted the coffee cup to have something to do that would take her eyes away from the scrutiny of her friend. She glanced at her name written on the cup in strong letters. She recognized David's printing. Someone at the coffee shop had not written that, but his own hand had inscribed her name. She wanted to drop her defenses and let him in, but there was so much saying it was a bad idea.

"Amber, I work for David."

"And…?" She gave her the look a second time.

"It's not a good idea to get involved with your boss."

"Tell that to all the secretaries and assistants who have married the guy they worked for."

"There are so many reasons why having a relationship with David is a bad idea. Suppose it doesn't work out?"

"Suppose it does?" Amber countered.

The two women stared at each other for long seconds.

"All I'm saying is give him a chance," Amber went on. "Give yourself a chance."

Rose thought about it. Her heart told her Amber was right. Rose was already attracted to David, more than attracted. She'd been in his arms, been up close and personal with what he offered her and knew how honorable he was when he refused to take advantage of a situation *she* would have gladly given in to.

"Think about it, Rose."

Before she could answer, footsteps echoed into the practically empty space. David and the two movers were back.

"Is that the end of it?" one of them asked, his gaze on a box in the corner.

"The final box," Amber said cheerfully. She stepped back, surveying the kitchen table and Rose.

"I'll put this one in my car," Rose said.

David took the box. They all filed out, leaving Rose to lock the door. She took a final moment to look back. She didn't think she would want to. The apartment represented a dark part of her life. She could almost see the ghost of herself moving through the space. The ghost could stay, she thought. That person no longer existed.

Rose closed the door and turned the key in the lock. She went down the stairs without a backward glance.

Three hours later, everything Rose owned had been moved, unloaded and placed in bright airy rooms that overlooked the ocean. The place was a sea of boxes. David had made a table out of them and the three sat on the floor eating a pizza Rose had ordered.

Amber stood up and stretched. "I'm afraid that's it for me. You'll have to finish on your own. I'm off to work and my muscles are going to pay for it."

Rose and David stood.

"Thanks, Amber. I know I can always count on you." They hugged. Amber waved at David and Rose walked her to the door.

"Remember what I said," Amber whispered. "Give him a chance."

Rose smiled as her friend left them alone.

"She didn't flirt as much this time," David said.

"She thinks we're a couple."

"Are we?"

"Are we?" Rose repeated.

Rose stood across from him, the width of two boxes

holding the remnants of discarded pizza separating them. She felt the entire width of the Atlantic was between them.

"I can't answer that. We need to define what that means."

"Do you want to?" he asked.

She didn't respond immediately. She didn't know the answer. "Not now. Not today," she finally said. "And don't ask me when. I moved today. I have to unpack and I have to get ready to go to New York."

David moved around the boxes and came to her. Rose took a step back.

"I think you should leave now," she said.

"No," he said. "I'm not leaving."

Rose's head came up and she looked him directly in the eye. "What do you plan to do? Watch me open boxes?"

"There's no furniture here, no dressers, no sofa. Where do you plan to put the things in these boxes?"

"I've ordered furniture. It arrives next week. Amber promised to take delivery since I'll be in New York."

"And where do you plan to sleep until then?"

She looked around and pointed to a box near the bedroom door. *Sleeping bag* was written on it.

"You're planning to camp out for a week?"

He said it like it was the most asinine thing he'd ever heard. Rose had roughed it many times in the past. She could do it for a few nights. She still had the army cot she'd gotten after being let out of the hospital. She wouldn't be sleeping on the floor.

"I've been in worse conditions," she said. "And it won't be a week, only a couple of days."

"But you don't need to. I'll get you a room in a hotel until your furniture arrives. It can be expensed since I've asked you to leave on such short notice—"

"No," she said, stopping him.

"You can't stay here with no place to sleep, living out of boxes."

"David, I'm not your problem or your charity case."

He stepped back as if she'd slapped him. "You think I look at you as a charity case?"

"I didn't mean that, at least not the way it sounded."

"Then how did you mean it?"

She controlled her voice, so it didn't sound hostile. "I mean I'm a grown woman. I can take care of myself. I don't need a hotel room. If I did, I'd have made a reservation. I'm not your child."

"You're damn right, you're not."

Rose didn't know anyone could move as fast as David did. In an instant, he was in front of her, close enough that their bodies touched. His hands clamped on both sides of her head and he pulled her mouth to his. This time there was no tender brushing of lips. His mouth took hers in total domination. He held her tightly, but not painfully. His tongue swept into her mouth, taking what he wanted without request or permission. Rose withstood it. She resisted for as long as she could, then joined in the kiss. As soon as she did, it changed. David relaxed a bit, making love to her mouth, not searing it with his own. His hands left her head and moved down her sides, brushing the sides of her breasts, causing waves of desire to course through her like a rocket launching.

The kiss went on. Each time Rose felt he was about to end it, his mouth would reposition itself, settling on another part of hers and beginning again as if he couldn't get enough of her. His hands followed the same routine, caressing her sides and back, running up and down in a continuous fever of denied need.

Finally, out of breath, they collapsed against each other. Rose forced herself to breathe normally.

"What was that?" she asked. "A show of your superior strength. Was the seduction included or just the brute strength? I'm no high-school girl trembling at the appearance of a guy she has a crush on."

"So you have a crush on me."

"We're not changing the subject. The point is you think you can force me to bend to your wishes with a simple kiss?"

"You think that kiss was simple?"

He was baiting her and she didn't like it.

David took a step forward. There was only a little space between them and he'd just decreased it by half. "Did you forget that you were in my arms? You were part of that kiss, simple or not. You were matching me tongue for tongue."

Images of them kissing, with no space, not even air, between them threatened her resolve. Her stomach felt as if it would turn over or, worse, she'd fall into David's arms as he was suggesting.

He grinned, something she wasn't expecting. "Is it working?" he asked.

"Is what working?"

"Your memory. Your body. Is it pumping passion juice through and you want to continue what I started?"

Rage burned through her. Rose kicked her foot through his legs, twisted one of them, hooking it over his calf. He lost his balance, going down on the unpadded, rugless, hardwood floor. His hard body hit it with a decided thump.

"Take that as my answer," Rose said, feeling fully superior to anything he could do, but also keeping out of his reach and the lightning movements she knew were part of his repertoire.

Monday morning dawned too early. David hadn't slept well since he'd left Rose's new apartment Saturday afternoon. He was losing his mind over her. He'd never acted like this before, like a crestfallen idiot. Why had he thought kissing her like that was a good idea? The truth was he hadn't thought. Where she was concerned his logical mind abandoned him.

She was going to New York this morning, so he'd have at least a week's reprieve before he had to see her. He knew he had to apologize for his actions. She hadn't been totally correct with her accusations toward him. She turned him on, pushed his buttons to the point that leaving her was painful. In the back of his mind, he didn't want to take her to a hotel. He wanted to take her to his place, have her sleep in his bed. He wanted to wake to her hair covering the pillow next to his.

He'd botched that good and well.

Why would she move to a place before her furniture arrived? She had nothing there, not even a bed. He couldn't imagine her in a sleeping bag like some camper. There wasn't even a chair or a table for her to have coffee on in the morning. There were only the boxes and not many of them. She'd lost everything in the storm. He knew that, but why wouldn't she order her furniture first and why wouldn't she stay with a friend for the few days until it arrived. He was sure Amber would have given her a bed for two nights.

Rose was an enigma. She'd been that way since the first day he'd seen her. He wanted to know her, wanted to get into her mind and understand how she thought. Yet each time he felt he might have taken a step forward, he'd do something stupid and fall back a mile.

David was an early riser, but today he didn't get dressed and leave for the office until well after nine. He knew Rose wouldn't be there. Melanie would be handling things and Rose was happy with her performance.

When he opened the office door, the place was empty. Melanie was at the store. The whiteboard had been replaced with computer electronics, thanks to the new assistant. Rose's perfume wasn't in the air and he missed it. Taking a deep breath he went through to his office, left his unopened briefcase on the desk and looked out the window at the new store. It was complete. They'd be moving in next week, as soon as Rose came back. Funny, he thought, how everything seemed to revolve around her.

His cell phone rang. David pulled it out of his pocket. He didn't recognize the number, but thinking, no, hoping, it was Rose, he answered it. The other party hung up as soon as he spoke.

"Guess it wasn't her," he said to no one.

Then he punched in a number. It was three hours earlier in California, but David ignored the time difference.

"Blake," he said when his brother answered on the first ring. "Sorry to call so early, but I thought you'd be up by now."

"I am up and I'm here."

"Here? Where?"

"I'm in New York City, getting ready to go to the store."

"What are you doing there?"

"Semiannual meeting with Mom and Dad. Don't you remember?"

"Oh, yes." David forgot they each had scheduled meetings with their parents. His meeting wasn't scheduled for another month. It would happen just before the store opened.

"Why don't you come up tonight? We could have dinner."

"You mean you have a free evening?" David laughed, remembering his brother and his penchant for always having a pretty woman on his arm.

"I know what you're thinking," Blake said, breaking into his thoughts. "I'm a changed man."

"Really, is there a woman who's caused this change?"

"No one in particular."

David laughed. He decided to leave that one alone. "I'll see you tonight about six."

The two agreed and he hung up. There was a stack of invoices on his desk he needed to go through.

David had planned to work in the office during the morning and spend the afternoon at the legal-aid center. Blake had him changing his plans. He decided to skip the invoices and the rest of the day. He was going to go home, pack a bag and head for New York.

Stopping by Melanie's desk, he told her he would be away a couple of days and confirmed which hotel Rose was staying in.

Three hours later he got off the train at Penn Station. His heart seemed to beat to the rhythm of the train wheels. He was in New York.

And Rose was in New York.

Rose paused as she stepped through the doors of Thorn's New York store. She'd been there before, but today it seemed different. Four steps led down to the main floor. Standing at the top, she surveyed the space. It was massive. Huge chandeliers hung in a straight line from front to back. Display cases were set in patterns of circles, mirroring the lights above them.

She understood what David meant when he'd explained the traffic flow. It felt like ages ago when he first came to Logan Beach and she'd thought he was changing everything, taking everything away from her.

She loved the store and this was only the first floor. There were eight other floors, plus the corporate offices. Rose wanted to meet the owners and managers. She had no appointment, but she took the chance they could see her for a few minutes.

The third floor was where the bridal department was. It was the same in the Logan Beach property. Rose walked through the area, her hand fanning through the gowns hanging there.

"May I help you find something?" a woman asked. "You have the glow of a bride."

Rose smiled, tears misting her eyes. No one had ever said that to her. She'd dreamed of her wedding, like any normal woman. "I'm not looking for anything," she told her. "Are you the department manager here?" She indicated the bridal department.

She nodded. "Been here ten years," she said. "I can usually spot a bride at twenty paces. And you've got the look."

Rose looked down and composed her features, before looking back at the woman. She was tall and slender, wearing a gray dress that flared at the waist and a light pink scarf. Rose understood that she didn't want her clothes to upstage a woman wearing a bridal gown.

"I'm the assistant manager of the store that's opening in Logan Beach. I'm in the city on a buying trip and thought I'd stop in and see the original store."

"Lannie Wagner," the woman introduced herself.

"Rose!"

Someone called her name. She turned to see a man who she didn't know striding toward her. There was something familiar about him. He reminded her of... David.

He shook hands with Rose and looked at the department manager. "Hi, Lannie."

"Good to see you again, Blake," she told him. "I didn't know you were back."

"Only for a meeting."

"It looks like you and…" She looked at Rose, who realized the two had never exchanged names.

"Rose Turner," she said.

"Rose is here to view the store," Lannie said.

"Well, let me be your guide," Blake said.

Another customer came into the department and Lannie excused herself.

"Do I know you?"

"Only by telephone," he said. "I'm Blake Thorn."

"How did you know who I was?"

"I talked to you on the phone. I have an ear for voices."

"I've never heard of that," Rose said.

"It's like some people can hear a song and immediately play it. For me it's a voice. I hear it, remember it and can identify it."

"You should be with the FBI."

He shook his head. "They've tried to recruit me, but I refuse them every time."

"Impressive," Rose said. "I wouldn't think many people refused the FBI."

"I like what I do and eavesdropping isn't my thing."

"What are you doing here? I thought you were in San Francisco."

"I'm here for a meeting. We have a semiannual meeting with the corporate heads." He gestured goodnaturedly when he said "corporate heads."

"Your parents," she said.

Blake nodded. "What are you doing here?"

"I'm on a buying trip in the city. I stopped by to introduce myself."

"Well, come with me." Gallantly, he offered his arm.

They walked to the elevator and as the doors opened on the top floor, she was greeted by a long wall of glass offices that bathed the entire area in sunlight. Blake turned right and headed for the end of the hall. Through more glass doors was the reception area for his parents' offices.

Greeting the two assistants sitting on opposite sides of the room, he was told they were waiting for him. Blake headed for the conference room that separated one office from the other.

He opened the door and Rose preceded him. The ready smile she had froze when her eyes locked on one man sitting at the polished table.

"David!"

Chapter 9

David stood up, looking from Rose to his brother. How did those two get together? And what was she doing here?

"I see the gang's all here," Blake said, cutting through tension he may not have known existed.

The last time David had seen Rose was when he left her in her new apartment after their devastating kiss and its aftermath. It hadn't been that long ago, but it felt like an eternity to him. He wanted to run around the table and kiss her. Only his parents' presence kept him stationary.

"Dad, Mom, this is Rose Turner, the assistant manager I've told you about," David said.

"Hello." Rose approached them and shook hands.

David looked at his mom. Katherine Thorn was almost as tall as her sons. Her hair was totally white and the style she wore made her look younger than her years.

"Call me Don," his father, Donald Thorn, told Rose. The two men had similar tastes and David noticed his father's suit almost mirrored his.

"I'm here on a buying trip and wanted to meet you before returning," she explained.

"David has told us a lot about you and how well you're managing the changes. Thank you," Mrs. Thorn said.

"You're welcome. I won't interrupt any longer. I know you have a meeting scheduled."

She was retreating. David could tell. He wondered if she wanted to get out of the room because he was there or if the memory of their last meeting was foremost in her mind.

"I have to go, too," David said. "It's Blake's show."

Both his parents looked at him in surprise. He'd agreed to stay for the meeting, but Rose's arrival changed that. He was thankful neither of them called him on it.

"We're still on for dinner tonight," Blake stated. "The pub at six."

"I'll see you there."

Rose said goodbye and headed out of the room, her back as straight as a board. If she could have gotten to the elevator before him, he was sure she'd let the door close in his face.

"Still angry?" he asked when he reached the hall.

"Angry, why should I be angry?"

He sighed. She wasn't going to make this easy. "Would it help if I apologized?"

"Are you sorry?"

"I am."

"Accepted."

"You say that like you don't mean it."

"David, what are you doing here? If you wanted to check up on me, why did you send me here alone?"

The elevator doors opened and they stepped inside. Rose punched the ground-floor button, hitting it several times as if that would make the door close faster. He took it as a sign that she wanted to get away from him as hastily as she could.

"I'm not here to check up on you."

"Than why are we both here when you asked me to come and do the buying?"

"I spoke to Blake this morning and since he's here for his report, we agreed to get together for dinner."

"And that's all?" she asked.

Of course it wasn't. He sent her here to put some space between them, but once she was gone, he missed her, missed the scent that wafted through the air when she'd been there, missed her smile and her presence. He even missed seeing her handwriting on the whiteboard they used to show their locations. He liked knowing where she was. Maybe that was the problem. He'd pushed his way into her life from the very beginning.

"Not exactly," he finally answered.

The elevator doors opened and they exited.

"What else?" she asked.

"You," he said.

Rose stopped in the middle of the jewelry aisle. She looked up at David, her expression perplexed.

"I didn't like how things ended the other day." He paused, hoping she'd say something, but she didn't. "When Blake called, I thought it was a good opportunity for us to get together away from the office."

"I have a meeting this afternoon and several others for the rest of the week. Don't worry about the argument. You apologized. I accepted it. Let's forget it and go on."

David didn't want to be in the same city with her and not see her. "You have to eat. Maybe we can at least meet for a meal. Dinner tomorrow?"

Rose took a moment to think about it. "All right, dinner tomorrow."

David held his smile. "Would you like me to go with you to the vendors?"

She was shaking her head before he finished the question. "You'd better go back to the meeting with your parents. I saw the look on their faces when you said you weren't staying. Obviously they expected you to."

He did smile then. "Very observant," he said.

"See you tomorrow," she said.

"How about a drink tonight?"

"You're going to dinner with your brother. I'm sure you two have a lot of catching up to do. I'll see you tomorrow."

"Tomorrow," he said.

David argued cases in front of hostile judges and juries that were clearly against him and won them over. But with Rose, he couldn't seem to crack her.

But that didn't mean he wouldn't keep trying.

The day had been exhausting. Rose was glad to be getting back to the hotel. It was only another block away. One of the vendors was obviously courting Thorn's for additional business. They'd offered her dinner and she'd accepted. It was better than being alone in her hotel room wondering where David was. After all the courses and glasses of wine, it was nearly ten o'clock when they broke up. All she wanted now was a long soaking bath and a good night's sleep.

She found treasure when that vendor offered to put in a large order when the store opened. She hoped David would be pleased. He'd said they were on the same wavelength. That was until she moved into her new apartment. She was unsure where they stood now and equally unsure of where she wanted the relationship, if that's what she could call it, to go. Her policy of not getting involved with colleagues was useless whenever David looked at her.

To think that he was somewhere in the city right now. She could be with him. She could have agreed to meet him for a drink. Why didn't she? It was only a drink—harmless. He was probably finished with dinner by now, but maybe the brothers decided to make it a night by visiting old haunts. It was an olive branch David had offered. Rose had thrown it in his face.

Amber's argument came back to her. Did Rose really push relationships away? Had Greg's death changed her so much that she feared ever feeling anything again? That couldn't be true because she felt something for David.

Reaching the hotel, she pushed through the doors and entered the lobby. The place was alive with activity. There was a party going on and many of the guests had spilled out into the lobby. Rose looked at the beautiful gowns the women wore. The men's suits and her previous meeting with David's parents reminded her of the way David dressed. It seemed everything reminded her of him.

Threading her way through the crowd, she entered a free elevator and pushed the button for her floor. Just before the door closed, a man slid through the opening.

"David!" For the second time that day he surprised her by being someplace unexpected. "What are you doing here?"

He pulled a plastic key card from his pocket. It bore the logo of the hotel.

"You have a room in this hotel? Why?"

"Closest to the store…" He paused. "Do you want me to leave?"

The door opened. They looked at each other, but neither moved to exit. "This is my floor," Rose said. She stepped out.

David stepped out. "This is my floor."

Rose only stared at him and began walking down the hall. David's footsteps were barely audible on the carpeted hallway, yet Rose could feel more than hear them. "Are you following me?"

"No," he said.

"Where is your room?" she asked.

"Next to yours."

Rose stopped abruptly. David plowed into her. She twisted out of arms that surrounded her and faced him.

"Why?"

"Would you like me to move to another hotel?"

Indecision wavered in her. "No," she whispered.

David made a sound that was indescribable. Then, with another of those lightning moves, he was by her side and she was in his arms. Rose didn't know how they got into his room. They could have moved through solid wood and she'd believe it.

David cradled her close, holding her as if she was the most precious thing in the world. For a long time after he closed the door, they stood in the same spot, their arms wrapped about each other, breathing in their scents. Rose couldn't believe how much her heart had swollen when she saw him in the conference room of the Thorn store. Now, with his arms around her, she felt as if it took up all the room in her chest.

Soft lips pressed into her temple. She turned toward his mouth, seeking. The kiss to her temple had been calming, a good-night kiss—as if she was going to sleep. She drew closer to it, turning her face until their lips connected and pressed together in a kiss so sweet, she thought it couldn't be happening to her. David's hand smoothed her hair and she moved her cheek to connect with his.

Hands moved over her back, drawing circles that created fires in places they did not touch. David's mouth moved to her cheeks, her ear and back to the corner of her mouth. Rose felt a strong need grip her. Hands touched her face, slipped into her hair as the kiss inched back closer to her mouth. She waited for it, anticipated it. Her mouth was dry with wanting and her body flamed. She needed to feel him, all of him.

"David," she whispered, her voice a raw ache. He was there. This wasn't a dream. She'd dreamed of David holding her so many times, but he was here, and the heat around them was hotter than any she'd imagined.

Warm hands slipped down her arms. Her body started a slow burn. The soft pads of his hands brushed over her breasts. She moaned aloud, arching toward the pleasure-giving palms. Finally, his mouth took hers again. A hand in her hair held her to him as he branded her mouth, sealed it with his own private insignia. The kiss was passionate, as consuming as an erupting volcano. She opened her mouth as his tongue slipped inside. He tasted wonderful. A thrill spiraled through her and she was lost to compete with the rage-awakening emotions he stirred. Rose's arms encircled him, threading into soft, springy hair and holding his mouth to hers as she performed her own private duel. How was this happening? How could David make her body so pliable? She felt as if she would melt and only her skin was keeping her form intact. Rose wasn't dreaming. Something more elemental was happening to her, to them.

It was primal. A jungle beat sang through her veins. She could hear the steady beating of a drum, or was it her heart? She couldn't tell.

She wanted to question David, but couldn't. For a moment he pulled away. She gasped, trying to close the distance between them. He pulled her to the bed. Piece by piece he removed the suit that had been so crisp at the beginning of the day and now looked as if she'd run through a rain forest. He looked at her in the moonlight filtering through the windows. Rose did not flinch or feel naked. She wore her underwear, but David's gaze was on her shoulders. He followed the gaze with his hands, running them over her skin. Rose felt the light weight of his fingers as they pulled each strap of her bra free and unleashed her breasts to his waiting hands. Her eyes closed as his thumbs rubbed her nipples to lift. Sensation spiraled through her.

She wanted him and she didn't want to wait. She pushed his jacket off his shoulders and unbuttoned his shirt. Her fingers splayed across moist skin and she pressed her lips to it. She inhaled deeply, taking in the smell of him. David's hands drove into her hair as she moved farther and farther down the trail of buttons.

In seconds, they were clawing at each other's clothes, removing them until their bodies were silhouettes. He kissed her again, pulling the covers back and lifting her onto the sheets. Slowly he deepened the kiss, his hands running over all the skin he could reach.

David moved over her until his length was fully her length. Rose accommodated his larger body in the well of hers. Need ran through her until she was clawing at his back. David quickly sat up. Rose heard the tearing of the condom foil and felt David protecting them. Then he was back with her. Pure sensation enveloped her at the feel of his hard physique against her softer one.

Clamping her teeth over her lower lip, she suppressed the scream of pleasure that boiled inside of her.

Logic and coherency reared like a flash of sanity but were quickly incinerated by the burning furnace that raced through her. She scraped her fingernails down his back, feeling the bumpy column of his spine. As she gasped for air, he dug himself into her parted thighs; the groan of pleasure escaped her before she could stop it. His mouth came back to hers, producing a mind-numbing sensation. His legs straddled her, shifting his weight to the mattress on either side of her. He pulled her up, keeping his mouth firmly fastened to hers.

There was no space between them. Air would even have a problem finding room. Skin from skin, mouth from mouth, lover from lover, they stroked each other, pleasured each other, bore each other to sexual frenzy. David held her in a sitting position. His arms spanned her body in a tight grip as his mouth mapped a slow and deliberate route over her face and down her neck. Rose, lost in sensual ecstasy, dropped her head back, accepting the sensual delight he chose to give her. Slowly he pressed her back until she felt the warm sheet under her. Her body throbbed with excitement. His mouth covered one breast, teasing it to a hard nub; teeth bit into the delicate skin and he explored each inch of skin from her breasts to her abdomen. Her breath caught in her throat as her hand gripped the muscles of his shoulders.

"David," she called again, an anguished plea in her voice. Her back arched. Her fingers dug into his flesh as she held him in place, allowing the tremor rioting through her to last as long as she could stand it. David persisted with his test of her endurance as she writhed beneath him. She was hot, raging and ready. Yet he wouldn't stop his tenacious quest for the volatile explosion that was imminent.

His wet tongue circled her navel. She whimpered, reaching for him, clamping onto his shoulders. His mouth moved farther down, over her belly, her inner thighs and finally the core of her being. A scream escaped her, cut short by the swift movement of David as his length covered her and he took her mouth.

"Now, David," she demanded, her breath ragged and short against his lips. "I can't wait any longer."

David wasn't ready to put her out of her exquisite misery. He drove her further toward insanity, rotating his hips against the soft stretch of skin that throbbed for attention.

She cried out, reaching for him, her body a furnace of pliant flesh. She muttered incoherently, sinking her teeth in his shoulder.

Spreading her legs farther, she linked them behind him. Still he refused to enter her. Rose went mad with need. Her stomach coiled into tight knots.

Rose! God, Rose! She heard the raw savagery of her name as David joined with her, slipping easily between legs that opened to receive him. Rose thought she would die as the wild cry of rapture seized her. David was a relentless lover, as exciting and terrifying as free-falling through space. He took her hard and fast, as fast as she demanded. She had no control; sensation and need ruled her actions. David completed her. They were one together, a single unit without beginning or end. She had not known such completeness could exist. He was the extension of her and she was part and parcel to his being. A bond linked them together; stronger than anything she had known. Nothing could break it. They were joined.

Rose moved with him, learning his rhythm, teaching him hers. She touched him wildly, uncontrollably, every part of their bodies attached. Her hands pushed, pulled, caressed, taunted, teased. She wanted to touch him all at once, know every inch of his strong, muscular frame.

He gathered her closer, lifting her higher and higher until the strain was unbearable. On a harsh cry the world exploded. Millions of fragments floated in slow motion around them. Light hitting the remnants changed them into a dash of color. Rose fell over the edge, clinging to David as the final release broke the time rift and dropped her sweating body against the sheets.

The aftereffects were like shock waves. Her body quivered with the emotional release leaving her heaving in David's arms. She breathed hard against him, her heart thudding against her chest. Rose held on to him, raining kisses over his face and shoulders. Her arms and legs wrapped around him, holding him to her, savoring the feel of his body connected to hers. Madness still gripped her. She was still for countless minutes, until David shifted his weight and slipped into the space next to her languid figure. She felt as light as air and as heavy as iron. Her mind whirled with the sensation of the experience of making love, yet her arms were too heavy to raise above her head.

David wedged her body into his, spoon-style, and

cupped her breast in his hand. Rose smiled and murmured incoherently. A cocoon of euphoria enveloped her. She wallowed in it for an eternity before sleep claimed her.

David woke to the smell of Rose's hair. He took in the scent, refusing to open his eyes in case last night had been a dream and he was only imagining what he wanted it to be. She was warm next to him. Pressing his face farther into her hair, he snuggled her closer to him. She moaned, waking.

"What time is it?" she asked, her voice lower and languid from a night's sleep.

"Morning," he answered. "There are no clocks. We have all the time in the universe."

Still in the sleepy-time voice, she said, "Wouldn't that be wonderful?"

"Yes." He held on to the word, giving it a new meaning. It would be wonderful for them to spend the rest of today and all the tomorrows exactly as they were.

Rose twisted her head and looked at the clock. "Seven o'clock. I have a meeting at ten."

"Cancel it?" he asked.

She turned over, facing him, her knees knocking into his. He captured them, curling hers with his. Her arm circled him. His body reacted immediately, growing hard against her. David had no control where she was concerned and he knew it. He didn't try to stop his need for her, but pushed her on her back and kissed her hair, then her forehead, and proceeded down her face to her mouth.

He loved the sounds she made as he brought her body to sexual life. Rose's arms extended upward until they were above her head, while David's hands played over her skin like a maestro tuning a fine instrument. Rose's eyes were drowsy, half-closed, her breathing a staccato rhythm as his hands roved over valleys and curves. When he touched her already aroused breasts, she drew in a fast breath.

Her arms and legs moved at the same time and she wrapped herself around him. David looked down at her. To say the eyes were the windows to the soul was an understatement. He'd wanted to drown in those eyes since the first day Rose poked her head through the door of her dark apartment. Today he was doing it.

Quickly, he straddled her, pushing himself inside her and groaning at the pleasure that coursed through him on his entrance. His sounds mingled with hers to the point that he couldn't tell one from the other. Blood beat through his body. He was hot. She was hotter. His movements began as a slow beat, which quickly escalated into a desperate need. He drove into her, hard. Her body took his and matched it. Together they mated, clung to each other, holding on as the universe exploded.

David collapsed on Rose. He pushed himself onto his elbows to keep from crushing her. His breath was hard and heavy. Hers was the same.

"One of us has to get up and go to work," Rose said.

"Not if I stay here." He moved his hips, grinding them against her to prove his point.

"You want your store to open, don't you? You want it to be the best we can make it? Then I need to keep my appointments." She kissed his lips quickly and dropped her head back on the pillow. "And you need to go back to Logan Beach and see that everything is in place."

"Logic," he said. "I hate logic."

She laughed. He felt her stomach move against his.

"You're a lawyer. You live in logic."

"Not where it concerns you."

The moment was suddenly charged. David stared at Rose. Slowly, he dipped his head and kissed her lightly. He let time run as he dropped more kisses over her face. Then with a loud moan, he leveled himself up and rolled off her.

Rose got up. Her clothes were strewn all over the room. She gathered them and shifted into her skirt and top, leaving everything else bundled in her hands. She was the sexiest thing he'd ever seen, even more sexy since he knew nothing was under that shirt except smooth hot skin.

Chapter 10

Riding on air couldn't describe how Rose felt for the rest of the week. David didn't go back to Logan Beach, but spent each day working remotely on Rose's computer and each night in bed with her. Rose couldn't wait for the day's meetings and orders to be over so she could return to the hotel and spend time with him.

After a bad two-year stretch, it seemed the sun had finally come out on her world. Although she never figured it would be in the form of a tall, athletic-looking Adonis with broad shoulders and buns so tight women pushed their chairs back to gaze at him as he walked by.

And he was hers.

They rode the train back to Logan Beach, only separating when she went to her apartment and he went to his.

Monday morning dawned and Rose popped out of bed, ready to greet the day and ready to see David. Arriving at the office early, she checked the schedule and saw that David was in the store.

Melanie came in. "Welcome back. I thought I was going to have to hold down the fort all by myself."

Rose smiled. "David took an impromptu trip to see his brother. I had a lot of meetings. Here are the orders. We should expect the inventory within a week."

"I'll notify Receiving," Melanie said. She took the receipts from Rose and laid them on her desk. "By the way, did you see the Sunday paper?"

"I haven't had a chance to read it." Rose had been busy with the new furniture and boxes that had arrived while she was away. Melanie's comment reminded her of the story Jim South had written about Thorn's. David told her it was going to be in the Sunday paper.

Melanie handed her a copy. Rose took it, heading for her office. "Oh!" she gasped as she read the headline and beginning of the story. Melanie was right behind her.

"I was surprised to see it. I thought that was all done with."

"Apparently not."

Jim South stated she was the assistant manager of the new store that was formerly Bach's department store and now bore the name House of Thorn. Then he went on to update readers on her rescue and the loss of her fiancé.

"The phone's been ringing all morning with requests

for interviews," Melanie said. She extended her hand with a sheath of papers in it. "All from reporters."

Rose took them and dropped them in the trash can. "I don't want to talk to any of them."

"Talk to any of who?" David said, standing behind Melanie with a newspaper in his hand.

"Reporters," Rose explained.

"I've been on the phone since I woke up," David said. "The article isn't what I expected."

"Me, either," Rose agreed. "I never talked to Jim South."

"I did," David said. Both women looked at him. "I only mentioned your name when he asked who you were." He looked directly at Rose. "I thought he was attracted to you."

If Rose had been thinking clearly, she'd have appreciated the fact that he was possibly jealous, but thoughts of resurrecting her past life usurped that.

"I never thought he'd slant—" he held up the newspaper "—this article toward you."

"He's Jim South," Rose explained. "He's used to covering harder news than the opening of a new department store. I wondered what brought him here."

"Obviously, he knew about you," Melanie supplied.

"I don't think so," Rose countered. "He was surprised when he saw me. But I guess using me was a better story than the store." She looked at David. "I don't mean that the way it sounded."

"I know," he said. "I'm just concerned about you."

Rose smiled. "I've weathered worse. And that life is

behind me. From now on I'm living in the present and looking toward the future."

"What about the phone calls?" Melanie asked. "Should I tell them you're unavailable?"

"That will only make them more curious," David said.

"Well, I can't go away. I just got back. And that won't stop the phones from ringing. They'll just wonder where I am."

"She's right," David said.

"Got any ideas?" Rose asked the two of them. "I'm open to anything."

Neither of them said a word. Then the idea came to Rose. She turned and retrieved the messages she'd dumped in the trash can.

"What?" David asked.

"Melanie, call all of them and tell them I'll agree to their exclusive interview."

"Exclusive?" she asked.

"Exclusive," Rose repeated with emphasis. "Set it up for this afternoon, three o'clock, no other time. The interview is to be in the store. The entrance is ready. We'll have it there."

"What are you going to do?" David asked.

Rose smiled and then laughed wickedly. "I'm going to give them what they want."

"And what's that?" David's eyebrow went up in question.

Before Rose could answer, his cell phone chimed. He reached into his pocket and pulled it out. Then he looked up. Both women waited. The expression on his face turned to stone.

"Who is it?" Rose asked, fear entering her voice.

"My mother."

The cavernous room held everything except the merchandise. The chandeliers, display cases, rugs and entry doors were all in place. The general din of conversation came from the ten reporters who were all talking to each other and grilling Melanie on why the others were present for the "exclusive" interview. Stoically, Melanie remained mute.

David thought that this better be a good plan. He wasn't sure what it was, but Rose had assured them it would work. They'd have their story and the store would be publicized in a positive manner.

Rose entered from the back of the store. When the reporters heard her footsteps they all stopped talking.

"Please sit," she said, standing in front of the group without a microphone or podium.

The group sat down noisily.

David stood to the side, watching the crowd. Rose was also within his sight. Melanie moved to stand next to him. He felt as if everything had been choreographed. And the play was about to begin.

"Thank you for coming on such short notice," she began.

"I thought this was an exclusive," someone stated.

"It is," she said. "You are all welcome to an inside look at the newest jewel in the House of Thorn."

Rumbles went through the crowd. David smiled.

"First, you want to know about me. How I came to be the assistant manager here?"

"Yeah," the same voice said.

"It's no secret. The Bachs asked that the new store keep as many of the employees as possible. Mr. Thorn asked me to return and here I am."

"What about your rescue from the hurricane—any aftereffects?"

Rose raised her arms and turned totally around. "As you can see, my wounds have healed. Like all the survivors of the storm, we are a strong lot. We can't let something like the Atlantic Ocean get us down."

The crowd laughed. Every question that came was greeted with a humorous or direct answer. Rose had them. She'd turned their disappointment into camaraderie, friendship even.

"Now, if you'll follow me, I'll show you around the House of Thorn." They began to stand up. "And…" Rose's voice stopped them. "About those pictures of me being pulled from a collapsed building, be sure to show the before *and* after." Again she got a laugh out of the crowd. "I expect a positive story about this store and what it will mean to our community."

Eagerly the group followed. David and Melanie stayed where they were.

"I wouldn't have believed it if I hadn't seen it with my own eyes," Melanie said. "I think when I grow up I want to be like her."

"Me, too, Melanie. Me, too."

To say they breathed a sigh of relief after the reporters filed out was an understatement. David left to go to the legal-aid center. Rose went through the motions, but mainly the rest of the day was a blur. On her way home, David called and the two of them decided to spend the evening together. Rose's tiredness evaporated. Excitement and anticipation filled her.

She arrived at David's apartment. He swept her in the door with a kiss.

"You were amazing today," he said. "Those reporters were eating out of your hand."

"I hope they give us a positive slant to the stories."

"From what I heard, that's what we should expect. But let's put that out of our minds and celebrate."

"Celebrate?" she asked.

With his hand on the small of her back, David led her to the dining room. There was a rose on the center of the table, which was set for two.

"You prepared dinner."

"*Prepared* may be overstating the truth."

He'd bought all the food and put it in serving plates. The boxes and containers sat on the kitchen counter.

"It's the thought that counts. And I'm starving."

Rose realized she hadn't had anything to eat. She'd drunk coffee and bottled water, picked up a few peanut-butter crackers, but her adrenaline level had been too high for her to think of a meal.

"This was so thoughtful," Rose said, taking the chair David held for her. They ate and drank, enjoying the food and talking over what had happened in the store that day, other than the interview.

"I've been so busy," Rose told him as they moved from the table with cups of coffee. David's windows faced the ocean and they settled on his balcony, allowing the breeze to cool them. "I haven't asked how things are going at the law center. Are you enjoying working there?"

"I love it."

"It's been good for you," she said.

The two of them sat on a double-wide seat. Rose nestled against him, reveling in the feel of his hard chest.

"What does that mean?"

"You're different…happier." She shrugged, not fully explaining her meaning.

"I wasn't happy before?"

"Not like this. You were doing what needed to be done, but at night when you left the office, you only thought about the structure of the work, making sure everything was in its proper place."

"People are different. You can't put them in a place and expect them to stay there."

"I believe the people are the reason you like it. You like helping. And you like unpredictability."

David hesitated, then looked around the room. When his eyes came back to her, he said, "You're right."

"You can't have just figured that out. I'm sure you've been proud of your accomplishments when you've won justice for someone."

"*Justice* is a very difficult word in legal terms. Sometimes it's only in the mind of the winner. The loser always thinks it's unjust."

"But where you are, when you win, it's for someone who can't afford the best attorneys and can't see any other way of getting out from under a bad situation."

"Mostly," he said. Then he laughed. "I had an interesting case a few weeks ago."

Rose raised her head, giving him her full attention.

"A little girl, thirteen, wanted to divorce her parents."

"Divorce? Can you do that?"

"It's not called divorce. A child, even a minor child, can be emancipated from parental control. There are specific *circumstances* that must be met, like being self-supporting. This one is so major that a child would have to practically be an heiress to have it happen. Then there must be resources to support and manage their income."

"So as a rebellious teenager, you can't just dump your parents without good reason?"

"Very good reason."

"So what did you tell the thirteen-year-old?"

"First, I took her to lunch. The offices are not your standard mahogany paneled halls, but a large room with tables, a few movable cubicle walls and very little privacy."

That had to account for the way David dressed on those days. Sometimes he would come to the store after his day at the center. He wore casual pants and a short-sleeved shirt. Not the usual costume of the lawyer that Rose was used to seeing.

"I wanted to get at the root cause of her wanting to leave home. And by law I needed to know if there was any abuse involved." He looked up at her with a relaxed expression. "Thankfully, I found none."

"So why did she want to leave?"

"She felt her parents didn't understand her."

"What was the outcome?"

"She called them and they came and got her."

"Wait a minute, there's a huge section missing."

David smiled. "I asked her to tell me her story. And I listened. That's what she needed, someone to listen to her. I let her talk for as long as she wanted—two hours. By that time, she'd talked herself into staying. At last, she told me she didn't want a divorce."

"That's wonderful, Dr. Phil." Rose called him by the name of the popular television psychologist who could solve anyone's problems in his one-hour daily program.

"All my cases aren't solved with a hamburger and a plate of Coney Island fries, but it only takes one to keep me going."

"I understand. I love the store. When I wake up in the morning, going there invigorates me. It's not like going to work, more like going to a place where you can have fun every day."

"Exactly," David said.

"I don't know what would have happened to me if you hadn't come to my door that day. It changed my life."

David didn't say anything. She felt his chest heave a little and knew he was fighting emotion. His arms, already around her, pulled her closer and she felt his mouth kiss her forehead. Rose lifted her head for a full kiss.

She was happy, happier than she ever thought she would be. She had a job she loved and she had David in her life.

None of the papers waited for the Sunday edition. The stories appeared the next day and none of them used the before-and-after approach, as Rose assumed they wouldn't. Each reporter assumed someone else was doing it and, of course, no one did.

David came into her office and pushed the door closed. Rose stood up and he took her in his arms, giving her a long delicious kiss. "My mother loves you. Those stories will bring the world to our door."

"Glad to hear it," she said, leaning against him. "I missed you."

"Same here."

She pushed back. "Now that I have an ally in your mother *and* the newspapers, I'd better finish this job. The hiring is coming along. All the fixtures are in place and many of the departments are set up and ready. Melanie is directing the office move. That should be done before the day is over. The opening will be here before we know it."

"Okay," David said. "I'll go, but we'll meet tonight."

Rose smiled. "It's a date. You can help me move some of that furniture and open boxes."

"That's not what I had in mind," he said with a smile.

She grabbed her checklist and they left together, but headed in different directions once they got to the store. Rose headed to the bridal department. It was her favorite of all the areas of the store. The new department manager and several employees were there going over what needed to be done. Only one of them was from the old Bach's store. Rose knew they had offered most of the former employees new jobs, but some of them had already moved on and liked their new positions.

"Is everything ready to go here?" Rose asked the manager.

"Everything has been delivered and set up. We're ready to open."

Checking it off her list, Rose moved on. She did the same thing, department by department and floor by floor. As she was entering the receiving area to check on orders and make sure they had come in, she heard a familiar voice. Smiling, she went toward it, then stopped when she overheard a conversation.

"Don't worry about it. We'll be up and running before they know anything about it."

"Garth," Rose said.

He nearly jumped out of his skin.

"Is everything all right?"

"Sure, sure," he said. "I was just startled."

"Sorry, I didn't mean to surprise you. I see you got your old job back. Are Mary and Olivia here, too?"

"Both," he said. "They're in shipping and accounts."

"I wanted to check on some orders I placed while I was in New York. Mainly beach objects, bowls, statues, lamps, that sort of thing. They're from Cosgrove Enterprises. Have they come in yet?"

"I can check and send you an email. We've had so much coming in that we're a little behind in inputting all the data."

"Do you need some help. I can—"

"No," he said quickly. "We'll get it done. I'll go see to it right now."

"Thanks." Rose smiled. She wanted those pieces available the first day. It was good to have some things that said *beach* in a store set in a beach town. The standard beach towels, books on the locale and pictures of the area were already in place, but the unique items she bought had yet to be placed.

Rose ran into David when she went to the top floor to check their offices and to change her shoes to a more comfortable pair.

"How's it going?" she asked.

"I see we hired the three people I met at the coffee shop."

"I saw Garth in Receiving. He told me."

Garth's phone conversation came back to her. She wondered who he was talking to and what he meant. It sounded clandestine, but Rose knew her imagination could run away with her. She only heard one side of it and she was not prone to eavesdropping.

"Do you have any reservations about them?"

He hesitated a long moment and then said, "No."

"I'll change my shoes and see about the other departments. It looks like Melanie has this area under control." Rose glanced into David's office. "Except for your desk."

The desk was full of papers. David's sleeves were rolled up and his jacket hung on the back of his chair.

"I'm just doing some analysis."

"On what?"

"I'll give you a full report when I finish. Right now I'm in the middle of it."

He looked around and saw no one, then kissed Rose on the lips.

She went to the next department on her list and

continued checking until she'd gone through the entire store. By then it was well past time to go home. When she got to her new office, David was gone. His jacket was missing and his desk was clear of all the papers she'd seen there. He was probably out buying them some dinner.

Rose smiled at how thoughtful he was. Including being a fantastic lover, he was easy to talk to, sensitive and caring. She could imagine him in a courtroom appealing to a jury, giving them the same charm that exuded from his pores. How could they do anything other than bend to his will?

His car was also missing from the parking lot. Rose got into hers and drove to her apartment. An hour later, David had not appeared and hadn't called. She wondered what he was getting for their dinner. Using this much time, it had to be more than a pizza. She was hungry. She picked up her cell phone and dialed David's number. He didn't answer. But there was a knock on her door.

She clicked off the phone and rushed to the door. Pulling it open, she said, "Did you get something special?"

"Very special," he said.

Rose knew by his tone that something had happened. She looked at him, but his face was hooded. He walked past her and into the box-strewn living room.

"David, what's wrong?"

He dropped a packet of paper on the top of a box. Rose picked it up and looked at them. She fanned through the lot.

"I don't understand. These are Bach's invoices from several years ago, most of them before the storm."

"And before that," he said. "I have boxes of them."

"Would you start at the beginning and tell me what these mean?"

"I've been looking at the books going back several years."

"Yes," she prompted.

"Is there anything you want to tell me about these?"

Rose picked up a handful and looked at them. "What do you want me to tell you?"

"You know nothing about these?"

"I don't understand. Why should I know anything about them? They look like normal orders."

"Appearance can be deceiving. These invoices don't have corresponding orders, yet there are payments for them."

"Maybe the orders are misfiled."

"They were never entered in the order-processing system, but they all have your signature on them." He lifted a paper and pointed to her signature. "Then there are the ones for the furniture in this apartment."

Rose was confused. The signature was certainly hers. She did order for the Bachs at times. When she looked at the merchandise, it could have been something she ordered. She didn't remember.

"I did use the company discount in ordering the furniture. That was something I reported at one of our staff meetings before I did it. And I paid for it."

"It doesn't appear that was all you ordered."

"David, you can't think I ordered stuff and didn't account for it."

"I find no accounting for any of these invoices and I have boxes of them."

"All with my signature on them?"

"Every one."

"I don't understand," Rose said. "I'll have to check on these tomorrow."

"There is no tomorrow," he said. "It would be best if you don't return to the store."

"You're firing me?"

"I think it's better than prosecution."

The door closed with finality as David left her apartment. Rose crumpled to the floor, her knees no longer able to support her. What had happened? How could he think she'd steal from the company? How had her name gotten on those invoices? She'd been a buyer at Bach's. Her name would have been on invoices back then, but she'd been assistant manger for three years. Her orders were few and only when she filled in for a buyer who may have been on vacation, or on an extended leave.

She had to get to the bottom of this. No one had ever called her a thief before and she wouldn't take it lying down. Getting up from the floor, she opened her laptop and immediately signed in to the store. Access Denied appeared on the screen. Rose tried it again, and again the same message came up. He'd locked her out.

She sat back, defeated. Things had been going so well. The store was coming through in her vision. She'd fallen in love with a dream man. She had a new apartment and new furniture and life couldn't be sweeter. Then, like Damocles' sword, her world had been split in two.

How could she defend herself? David hadn't even given her a chance. He'd gathered all his facts and they all pointed to her as the culprit. And now what was she going to do? She had an apartment to pay for, furniture to finance and no job. When word got out as to why she was looking for another position so soon after leaving the House of Thorn, she'd be unemployable.

What else could happen? Rose had lost everything. And now she could add her job along with the man she loved to the funeral pyre. Bach's was no more. The new department store was ready to open. House of Thorn would have a successful opening. In a few years, no one would remember Bach's, or that she was to be the store manager when the Bachs retired. No one would know she'd been the assistant manager at Thorn's Logan Beach, unless it was as a huge blemish on her record.

Rose refused to cry, although she wanted to. She sniffed, forcing her eyes to remain dry. There had to be a way to find out where those invoices came from. She knew the signature was hers, but she couldn't remember signing them.

There were only two people who could help her, or at least give her some guidance. Rose picked up her phone and called the Bachs. She arranged to have lunch with them the next day. She wished she could go over then and there, but restrained herself. The night went by minute by minute, each one dragging on as if it was an hour instead of sixty seconds. Sleep eluded her and the next morning she got dressed and began to get ready two hours before she was due.

Circles under her eyes and the tired look on her face reminded her of those photos Jim South used in his report on the store. What would he do now that she'd been fired? Spending her time using makeup to try and hide the blemishes, Rose hurried to finish getting ready, then left for the Bachs' house.

Forcing herself to drive slowly and rehearsing what she'd say, Rose knocked on the door of her former employers five minutes before the appointed time.

"Rose, what a delight to see you," Josie Bach said as she swung the door open and hugged Rose. "Come in."

Edward Bach looked tanned and younger than he had when he left the store. She supposed the pressure of running a department store had been relieved. His wife, Josie, had lost a few pounds.

"You two look great," Rose said, smiling.

"We joined a health club and Edward spends a lot of time on the golf course."

"While she runs after our grandchildren," Edward reported. He opened his arms and Rose went into them.

"We're so glad you called. We got our invitation to the opening and wondered how things were going for you."

Rose looked around the apartment. She'd been there many times for parties and dinners. The place was open-concept and had windows practically everywhere. Josie liked light. They were high enough to see the ocean, but their place had been spared the effects of the storm.

"Come on in, lunch is ready."

Rose followed them to the dining room. Their style was modern. The dining table was glass and the chairs were high-back velvet. They sat down to a fruit salad with yogurt topping followed by broiled salmon and broccoli.

When they got to dessert, Josie said, "So tell us what's happening. We saw the newspaper stories. It looks like things are getting back on track."

"We couldn't be more thrilled," Edward added.

"I've been fired," she stated.

Josie and Edward stared at her, each stopping whatever action they'd been performing.

"What?"

"Why?"

They both spoke at once.

"David has several years' worth of invoices with my signature on them. He says there are no orders to back them up. He all but accused me of theft. I honestly don't remember those invoices."

"Did you tell him that?" Josie asked, her voice that of a mother speaking to her child. Rose admittedly looked at Josie as a second mother.

"I tried, but he was in no mood to listen. Then I went to the computer to try and find out where they'd come from, but he'd locked me out of the system." Rose looked from one to the other. "Do you have any idea about what could have happened?"

A look passed between the Bachs that wasn't lost on Rose. "You do. You know something."

"No," Edward said. "Nothing we could prove. Every now and then a discrepancy in the accounts would come up, but it was quickly explained as a timing error. Those happen frequently in accounting."

Rose nodded. She knew that. "But for him to have boxes of invoices with my name on them. Something doesn't check out there."

"How can we help?" Josie asked.

"Then you believe me?"

"Of course we do," Edward said. "Thorn's isn't using the same programs we did for invoices, but we still have the ones that were off-site backups."

Rose's breath caught. "Do you think I could use them?"

"Not only use them," Edward said. "I'll help. It'll be good to get my hands back in the business, even if it's only for a little while." He glanced at his wife. Her smile was approving.

Rose exhaled. "I can't thank you enough."

"I'll have to get them out of storage. Why don't you come back tomorrow around one o'clock and we'll start."

"If I know you two, you'll be at this for a while," Josie said.

"I can't tell you how much this means to me." Rose felt tears in her voice. Emotion welled up inside her. Other than her family, no one had believed in her more than the Bachs, and they were on her side again. "I promise you, I did not embezzle money or merchandise from the store."

"We believe you," Edward said. "There's got to be an explanation. Don't worry, we'll find it. You're not the only one who wants to know the answer to that."

Chapter 11

David hadn't been able to sleep. At four o'clock he'd given up the fight and got up. By five o'clock he was on his way to the office. It was strange to enter the new building alone. He thought he and Rose would enter it together on their first day, a kind of crossing the threshold. He'd thought his life was changing in that direction.

With two cups of coffee in hand, he arrived at the executive offices at House of Thorn Logan Beach. There was an empty echo to the place as his footsteps tapped along the hardwood floor. His gaze went directly to the assistant manager's office. Rose wasn't there, of course. He didn't understand.

It made no sense. He'd held her in his arms, made love to her. She'd rocked his night and his world. Nothing had looked the same after that. She couldn't be a thief.

But those invoices.

Her name.

It was blatantly clear that if it wasn't her alone, she had to be in league with someone else.

Look at how he had found her, practically cowering in a dingy apartment. If she had money from a fencing operation, where was it, in a domestic bank or an offshore account? If so, why didn't she access it for living expenses? Why would she live in a badly furnished apartment and dress in clothes that were only serviceable?

It made no sense.

So what happened to the goods on these invoices? Who ordered them and where did they go? He turned and looked through the window. The sun had risen. The gulls were out looking for breakfast. He watched their flight paths in the distance, miles away at the water's edge.

It wasn't cold. But it was the light of day. Rose couldn't be guilty. There had to be another explanation. He was in love with her. He knew she couldn't do this. It made no sense. That refrain seemed to play in his head. It had been there all night, telling him over and over that he was wrong. He had to be wrong. The woman who'd shared his bed, who'd pulled his store, this store, into organization, couldn't be skimming off the top. It just wasn't in her. It wasn't in her makeup.

David reached for his phone. The boxes of invoices were stacked in a corner. Neatly printed labels outlined the range of dates. He dialed Rose's number. The phone rang several times, then went to voice mail. He hung up without leaving a message. He didn't know what to say. He'd accused her and refused to listen to her explain anything. What could he say over the phone? How could he tell her he believed in her? And why would she believe him?

How could he tell her he loved her?

Edward had set up the servers in his home office. Josie had a hand in the placement of the electronic machinery. Rose could tell by the way the room was organized and connected. Edward's desk, which had sat in the Bach's office for as long as Rose could remember, was now in this office. A second desk that had a chrome frame with a thick glass top had been moved in recently. Rose assumed it was for her.

The servers were on, providing a gentle hum as their fans kept the inner workings cool. Rose didn't ask how they got so much done in less than twenty-four hours. Edward had connections, plus he was a wiz with computers. He hadn't interfered with the information-technology department when he owned Bach's, but his training had been in computer systems and analysis. Edward had a passion for electronic technology and Rose knew it was hard to let go of something you loved.

"Ready?" Edward asked.

She nodded.

"When we got these installed, I pulled up some of the invoices to take a look and see if anything caught my attention immediately."

"Did you find anything?"

"Unfortunately, no."

Rose was disappointed. She hadn't expected this to be easy, but his comments gave her hope. "We'd better start sometime three years ago," she said.

"Why three years?"

"The ones David showed me were dated two years ago. By that time I was the assistant manager, no longer buying. Why would invoices be in my name when my approval would only be necessary if the order was over five hundred thousand dollars? The amounts on his invoices were five figures at the most."

She and Edward worked all day. Josie came in with meals and coffee at regular intervals, but they continued until Edward stood up and stretched his back. Rose realized they'd been at it for hours. It was nearly dark.

"Oh, I'm so sorry. I shouldn't have stayed so long."

Edward wasn't old. He was in his sixties, but sitting in front of a computer screen all day wasn't good for either of them.

"I'd better go," Rose said.

"You'll be back in the morning?" Edward asked.

"If that's all right?"

"Fine. Come early."

"About nine?" she suggested.

He nodded. Rose was usually at her desk by eight. The Bachs had always been in before she got to work. She didn't know if their patterns had changed since they'd retired.

"I'll have the coffee waiting," Edward said.

She said good-night to Josie and left. In her mind, she

continued to go over the invoices. Something seemed out of place, but then everything was out of place. She'd found invoices going back further than three years, but they were legitimate. The ones that made no sense began right after she was promoted.

"What happened then?" she asked the traffic in front of her as she drove. Unfortunately, it didn't answer her. What had happened at Bach's after she was promoted? Her position had been filled by another buyer, but that only lasted five months before the woman left due to her husband's transfer. Rose was still trying to come up with an answer when she opened the door to her apartment.

She was tired. Her shoulders hurt and she had a headache from sitting so long and leaning in to look at a tiny screen. But she wasn't sleepy. She should be. The last two nights she hadn't gotten much sleep, but her mind was active. She checked her phone, since she'd turned it off when she gone to the Bachs'. She had eleven calls, nine of them from David. Amber had called twice.

Rose deleted David's calls and returned Amber's.

"Well, it's about time," Amber said in place of a greeting. "Where have you been all day?"

"I'm working on a special project and I turned my phone off." Rose hadn't held anything back from Amber since the two of them shared the same hospital room. She didn't immediately tell her what project she was working on, or that David believed she'd stolen from the store.

"I saw the newspaper article. How'd you get that creep Jim South on your side?"

Both Amber and Rose had been targets in Jim South's original article. He'd reported their rescue, but cast some doubt on why they were in a place where a building could fall on them, as if it was their fault. Maybe that's why he'd been doing human-interest stories instead of hard news. Rose smiled for the first time that day.

"I got a new dress for the opening. I love the invitation. Who designed it?"

She cleared her voice. She tried to say David's name but it stuck in her throat. "The shop where we ordered them did the work."

"They're beautiful. I can't wait to go."

"Amber..." Rose paused, knowing she had to tell her. "I may not be at the opening."

"What?"

"The fact is I no longer work for Thorn's."

Amber didn't beat around the bush with questions. "I'll be right over."

Twenty minutes later her friend of two years walked through the door, dropped her purse on a box and went to the kitchen to open the bottle of wine she brought with her...with the wine opener that was on her key chain.

"Get a couple of glasses," she said.

"I don't know where they are. I have a coffee cup for the morning. Everything out here is still packed."

"We'll drink out of the bottle," Amber said.

Taking Rose's arm, she led her to the living room, where they took seats on the floor next to the still-covered sofa.

"Spill," Amber said, taking a drink.

"David believes I've stolen from the store." The words sounded so succinct, as if they were unimportant.

"The store isn't even open yet. How could you steal from it?"

"He's gone back into the invoices from the Bachs' store. He's found two years' worth of sales that never made the books."

"Why does he think you had anything to do with that?" She passed the bottle to Rose, who took a long drink.

"The invoices all have my name on them."

"That's what you've been working on all day," Amber said, showing her insight into reading what people say and what they mean. "Clearing your name?"

"The Bachs are helping me. Edward is letting me use his backup servers to try and track down what happened."

"Thank God for Edward."

Her cell phone rang. Rose didn't move. She assumed it was David again.

"You're not going to answer that?"

"David has called nine times. What could he have to say? He was very articulate two days ago. I have no need to listen to him."

"You mean you don't want to talk to him." Amber got up, picked up the phone and handed it to Rose. It was indeed David.

"You're going to have to talk to him sometime."

Rose clicked Refuse Call, turned off the phone and dropped it on the floor next to where she sat.

"Let him stew," she said.

"So, you're punishing him?" Amber asked.

"He deserves to be punished. He accused me of illegal activities and didn't give me the chance to deny or explain."

"You can explain?" Amber's brows went up.

"No, but I can deny."

They didn't finish the bottle of wine before Amber left. Rose put the last of it in the practically empty refrigerator and reminded herself she needed to buy some food. Now that she had more time, she could set up housekeeping while she looked for another job. She yawned, suddenly very sleepy. However, her headache was gone.

She picked up her phone and turned it on. Amber would call when she got in. Rose hoped David wouldn't try her again.

As she headed for her bedroom, there was a knock on the door. Looking through the peephole, she saw David standing there.

She gasped, clamping her hand over her mouth so she couldn't be heard. She stepped away, melting into the wall behind her. David knocked again. Immediately sober, Rose felt all the love she had telling her to open the door. She forced it back. They'd talked. He didn't believe her. He didn't trust her. Why was he here now? Maybe something happened in the store and he was here for her to fix it. Well, that was not going to happen. He could fix it himself or not fix it. In either case, she was not responsible.

"I saw your car, Rose. I know you're in there."

"Go away," she whispered, her voice only loud enough for her to hear.

"Rose," he called again.

"Go away," she shouted.

"I'm not leaving. I'll wake up all your neighbors if you want."

Rose was trapped. He knocked harder and called her name. She unlocked the door and opened it a crack. "What do you want?"

David pushed the door open and entered the apartment.

"Can't this wait until morning? I have a headache," she lied. She didn't know if the wine had taken care of that or her conversation with Amber. Usually, when she got something off her chest, she felt better.

"Maybe it could have if you'd returned my calls."

"I didn't see the point." She walked away, wanting to sit down, but realizing there was no place except the floor and she wasn't going to sit there.

"The point is I know I was wrong."

"You seemed pretty certain two days ago."

"Two days was more than a lifetime."

"Have you found out what really happened with those invoices?"

He looked at the floor then back at her. "No."

"So all the evidence still points to me?"

He didn't answer and that *was* an answer.

"Well, I guess we're done." She started for the door.

"Rose, I know it wasn't you. I can't believe you would do something like that."

"But you're not sure. Can you say there isn't a part of your mind that still wonders if I did it?"

"No one can say that, Rose."

"But I'm accused. And that shadow of doubt will be there until the ocean washes away all the sand on the beach—there will still be that grain of doubt." She used her thumb and forefinger to indicate a minute amount.

"I believe you're innocent."

"But you can't prove it, counselor."

He winced at that. She knew she was right and she knew she loved him. But there was nothing for them.

"It's not going to matter, David. If I couldn't prove my innocence, there is no way we can continue. The truth might make us friends, but we'd step around each other like polite strangers."

"Rose—"

"I think you should leave. And don't call me."

They stared at each other for a long moment. Then David went to the door. Rose turned her back so she wouldn't see him and so she wouldn't run into his arms, swearing her love and confessing that she wanted nothing more than to be with him forever.

The door opened. She waited, holding her breath, for it to close. David stopped. She could feel his eyes on her back, but she refused to turn and face him. She couldn't. Her energy reserves where he was concerned were almost depleted. If she turned she'd falter.

The door closed with a final click.

Rose sank to the floor and cried.

Friends. He'd take that if that was all Rose was willing to give. He was going to find the answer. He knew it wasn't her. He may have lost her with his accusation, but he would prove her innocent. He could find out if she would forgive him then, but he knew in his heart that whatever those invoices said, they had to be wrong.

It took him a week, but he thought he understood. He couldn't prove it, but he knew it was enough. To put the final finish to the proof, he needed to contact one more source.

He'd do that this afternoon.

At three o'clock, David walked through the doors of the Atlantic Arms condominium building and took the elevator to the top floor.

The last person he expected to see opened the door— Rose.

"What are you doing here?" they both asked at the same time.

"I have an appointment," David said and stepped inside. He wasn't giving her the chance to close the door in his face.

"David." Edward came forward, his hand outstretched. "It's good to see you again."

"You knew he was coming?" Rose asked.

"He called this morning and asked for a meeting."

Rose frowned. "And you allowed it."

Josie came over and stood next to her husband. "David," she greeted. Looking from David to Rose, Josie said, "Let's all go and sit down."

She led them to the large living room. The table in front of the sofa held a tray with coffee, tea and several types of finger sandwiches. David was instantly hungry, his body remembering it hadn't had much to eat in the last week. He passed the food and took a seat. Rose took a position on the opposite side of the semicircular sofa. Edward and Josie sat in chairs that faced them.

"David, do you want to tell us why we're here?" Edward asked.

David glanced at Rose. He hadn't expected her to be here, but he wouldn't have to convince her of his findings if she heard it firsthand.

"As I explained on the phone, I've been doing some research on the invoices that I found."

"You know Rose and I have been doing the same thing," Edward commented.

David was floored. "No, I didn't." He looked at her. She glared back.

"You didn't think I was just going to sit around and let you accuse me of theft and do nothing, did you?"

"What did you find?" Josie asked, apparently defusing the argument that was about to flare.

"I believe the invoices originated in the accounting department."

"That's where all invoices originate," Edward said.

"True, but they're triggered by an order that goes to the shipping department."

"You said these didn't have an order," Rose reminded him.

"They don't. And they aren't the same as the ones that come out of the invoice system."

"What do you mean?" Josie asked.

"The paper is different. I'd been handling them so long that I didn't have any real invoices. Only these fake ones. Last night, I picked up one of the invoices

Rose paid for the furniture she ordered. The paper felt different, so I pulled some old invoices from your files and indeed the paper wasn't the same."

"Someone printed the invoices and put my name on them?" she asked.

"That's my guess," David said. He hoped she'd look at him with softer eyes, but her face seemed to harden.

"Oh, my God!" Rose stood up, almost as if she was propelled from behind.

"What is it?" Edward asked.

"I know how it was done and I know who did it."

"Who?" Josie asked.

"One thing." She turned to David. "Have you told anyone you fired me?"

"I'm hoping I can convince you to come back, despite my accusation."

Rose ignored that. "What about Melanie?"

"I told her you had something personal to take care of."

"Good," she said. The old Rose was back, but David didn't know where she was going with her statement.

"David, can you access the Thorn system from here?" Rose asked.

"If there's a computer."

"Come on," she said, already moving toward the server room. The group looked after her before they all got up and followed.

David stopped in the door to an obvious office. This must be where Edward had said he and Rose were working. It was a virtual computer farm. The desks were littered with yellow pads, reminding him of his legal background.

Rose was in a chair, signing on to one of the machines. "Here, log in to the accounting system." She got up and moved to stand by the Bachs. Everyone looked confused. David did as he was told.

"Search on my name under authorization, using dates of the last three weeks."

"That will result in nothing," he said.

"Just do it," she told him.

He clicked several keys and hit enter. There should be nothing returning. In an instant the screen filled with three invoices. Behind him three people moved in, scouring the screen.

"That's impossible," David said. He swung the chair around and looked at her. "You haven't been in the office in a week. One of these invoices is dated two days ago. How is this possible?"

"Because the duo is back in business."

Chapter 12

The entire group went to the House of Thorn building. Rose went in first.

"Hi, Rose," Melanie said as she came out of her office at the sound of footsteps. "Everything okay? David said you were taking care of some personal issues."

"I got it under control," Rose replied.

"I haven't seen David much today. He went out before three, but didn't say when he'd be back."

"Fine. I'm expecting the Bachs in a minute." She looked at her watch for effect. "They wanted a private tour before the opening. Let's meet in the conference room."

"It'll be good to see them again."

Rose had barely gotten into her office before she heard the Bachs outside. Melanie's voice was happy and high-pitched as they greeted one another and talked about what was going on in their lives. Rose used the time to make a call. Then the couple joined her. Melanie and Rose outlined some of the changes that had occurred and what the Bachs would be surprised to see.

David came in and the hugs and greetings started all over again. It continued when Olivia, Garth and Mary arrived.

David closed the conference room doors and two guards took up residence outside.

"What's going on?" Garth asked. "Why are there guards here?"

"Take a good guess, Garth," Rose said. She picked up a paper that was on the credenza along the back wall and slid it across the table. "Recognize anything? Like my signature?"

Mary's face went white, then color rushed into it, turning her a deep pink.

"What is this?" Garth asked belligerently.

"It's the end of a research project," David said. "For years the Bachs wondered why they couldn't account for the 'timing' differences." He used air quotes to surround the word timing. "I thought Rose was involved since her name is on every one of these and the three boxes in my office."

"Without each other knowing, we've—" Rose used her hand to indicate David singly and herself and the Backs as a group "—been running the same inquiries and today everything fell into place."

"I don't understand," Olivia said.

"That's because you're not involved," Rose told her.

"You're my decoy. I invited you because the three of us had coffee together and these two wouldn't think they'd been found out if the three of you came."

Rose noticed her shoulders drop in relief.

"The way I see it," Rose continued, "the invoice originated in accounting, produced by Mary. I assumed you scanned a real invoice then changed what needed to be changed in order to make a template. We found the template on the backup system that the Bachs have."

Mary looked at the Bachs. They nodded. Edward held up a printed copy of it.

"No invoice number, no dates," Edward said.

"Next—" Rose took over again "—the order was called in not sent through the electronic system. Melanie signed my name to it and mailed it."

She gasped, surprised that she was being accused as part of a conspiracy. "I wouldn't do that."

"I remember once seeing invoices on your desk with Rose's name on them. You had a pen in your hand and told me they were for the office equipment she'd ordered," Josie said. "You acted very surprised when I came in the office."

"Those were for office equipment."

"I'm sure some of them were," Josie said. "But maybe there were one or two in there that had nothing to do with the equipment. Maybe there were one or two with a manual number different from the rest?" Josie's voice was soft and motherly.

"When the merchandise arrived, it should have been received by Garth, but it was delivered to a warehouse somewhere else. Am I right so far?" Rose asked.

She looked from one to the other. Their faces told the story.

"We've called the police. They should be here by now. We're turning over all the evidence," David said.

"You don't want to have us arrested. Think of what it will look like when we tell the press our story. No one will want to shop at your brand-new store," Mary said.

"First, you're guilty and I'm sure we can send you a reporter who'll slant the story the way you want it about how you stole for years," Rose said. "I'm willing to give Jim South a call myself. He can give you the same type of treatment he gave me."

"The House of Thorn is not having you arrested," Edward stated. "Bach's department store is the plaintiff. You stole from us for years and unlike the current computer system, the backup servers kept everything, even files that were created and erased in the same day."

At that point the police arrived.

Rose left the office and went home. She called Amber to give her the news, then went to bed and slept like someone who needed to make up for a sleepless week. When the sun woke her the next day it was mid-morning. She was ravenously hungry. She'd have to begin her job hunt soon, but today she felt totally free. The weight of accusation had been removed from her shoulders.

Going to the kitchen, she opened her refrigerator and looked at all the food that it contained. Milk, eggs, water, juice, everything she could buy in the grocery store and then some. She found a frying pan and her dishes. She was going to make a big breakfast and spend the day on the beach. When she got a job, Logan Beach would be a great place to work, but most of her time would be spent inside an office building or a store.

Sitting down with her food, she tasted the hot cakes with syrup and was immediately transported to her mother's kitchen for their Sunday morning meal. The smells of the room bathed in sunshine came back to her. She smiled at how they used to laugh and talk over meals. She missed her mom, but she now thought of good memories, not the images of her in pain as she suffered through her cancer. She wondered if today was the day she really began to accept and heal. All the losses that had happened to her could have put her on a road to destruction, but David had come along and forced her to look at life.

Life was beautiful. Without a job or a love, she could still see the promise it held.

Her phone rang. It was in the bedroom. Rose put the last bite of her bacon in her mouth, then took her coffee cup and went to answer it.

"What time will you be here?" David said. No "hello," no "how was your night?"—just "why aren't you here?"

"I don't plan to come at all. Did you forget, I don't work there?"

"You were never fired."

"It really looked like that."

"The opening is in two days. If you don't come here, I'm coming there." She could hear the humor in his voice. The old David. The David she fell in love with. The David she would always be in love with.

"Rose, would you come back to work for Thorn's? We need you. I need you."

Her heart melted.

"How do I know the next time you find a strange-looking invoice, you won't accuse me of theft?"

"Scout's honor," he said.

She could almost see him raising his hand with the three-finger salute.

"I promise to trust you forever."

Rose grabbed her chest at the swell of emotion that almost poured out of her at his words. She loved Thorn's and she loved David. Taking the store from her was like cutting off her fun for life. She wanted to go back. Even if there was no them to return to, no couple, she still wanted to be there.

"Give me a couple of hours," she said over the lump in her throat. "There's something I have to do first."

Rose sat for a few minutes after she ended the call. She was too happy. She was going back to the place she loved. She knew things had changed. Life would be different, but in time they might become more than friends. She wouldn't expect anything more now. It was enough that he trusted her.

Standing up, she went to her bedroom and opened the jewelry box. She hadn't looked at it in a long time, but today was a day for change. Rose opened the small blue velvet box. The diamond engagement ring sat against a white background. She was mesmerized by the setting. Memories of her gaping over the size when Greg gave it to her came back. Taking it out, she slipped it on her ring finger. It felt heavy, strange, since she hadn't placed it there for nearly two years.

The phone rang again. This time it was Amber.

"Amber, I don't have much time. I have to get to work."

"Work?"

"Oh," Rose said, remembering she hadn't updated her friend on all that had happened. "I'll tell you all about it later. Right now, know you have a place to wear that dress."

"You're back at Thorn's?"

"I'm back at Thorn's."

"And David?" Amber said.

"Maybe not David, but I have a job."

"A poor substitute for a man," Amber replied.

"He didn't trust me. He thought I was the culprit."

"And he spent more than a week proving you weren't."

"I had a hand in proving my own innocence," Rose told her.

"And David put his entire store on hold to find who was setting you up. Even if he did accuse you, his behavior spoke of other things."

"Are you implying that I am the one putting obstacles to my love life again?" Rose asked.

"You said it, I didn't."

"Well, there's one obstacle I'm about to remove."

"What's that?"

"The beach house. I'm going back to where this all started."

* * *

Wearing tennis shoes with her business suit, Rose approached the place where her home once sat. The numbness that overtook her in the past wasn't there. Her heart beat faster in her ears the closer she got to the lot. Footsteps that faltered the last time she ventured down this street didn't hesitate.

The house was gone. She knew that. She'd seen it the day she got out of the hospital. There were broken windows, burned, wet and mangled wood together with crushed and broken bricks, one kissing the other as if they were lovers tangled together, inseparable in their need for each other.

All that had disappeared. Only the slab of concrete that once led to the double wide doors remained intact. In the distance she heard hammering. Continuing, she walked to the front of the building. Stopping, she stood mutely in front of her home. In her mind, she rebuilt the house. Floor by floor she put the structure back together. The white painted colonial with huge round columns lifted into the air. One last time she would see it as it had been in its glory.

Her room had been on the back side, facing the ocean. She imagined the front doors opening, the same way Rebecca had dreamed of returning to Manderley in a long forgotten classic that had been on her bedside table and it too was taken by the storm. The wide staircase was visible as it led from the second floor down to the main level. Rose had come down that staircase in a long white lace dress the night of her cotillion. Aaron Milsap waited for her, uncomfortable in his tuxedo and carrying a wrist corsage still in the clear plastic container. His fingers were all thumbs as he tried to slip it over her hand.

As a child, she'd played in the foyer and bounded down the back stairs to run to the ocean and spend the day in the sun. All gone now. Yet it was only a building: wood, brick and glass. Her memories remained. She could see her mother sitting at her computer, watch her father teaching Rose to play chess when she was seven years old.

Greg had proposed to her in the living room in June. Neither suspected the devastation that was to come. She looked at the ring on her finger. For a long moment she gazed at it. She'd loved Greg, expected to spend her life with him. The ring was a tangible reminder. Yet, she didn't feel sad. She felt his love and knew he would understand that she had to remove it. Rose took off the ring. She held it in her hand and closed her fingers around it.

Then she opened her purse and put it in the zippered compartment, a goodbye gesture. Rose smiled at the thought. Her life didn't flash before her. She pulled it into perspective, taking each memory and giving it a safe place in her heart. Around her the sound had ceased without her notice. Then it came back. The house disappeared from her mind. The empty lot was there, but she didn't fear it. New construction was taking place. People were rebuilding.

Turning to go, she glanced down at a small flower that pushed up through the dark earth. Life renewing itself, she thought, and walked away.

* * *

Rose's car pulled into the parking lot and David's heart lurched. He headed for the employee entrance. Amber had called to tell him she was going to the beach house. He knew the reaction she'd had there before and it took all his resolve not to dash out the door and go to her. But he knew this was something she had to do alone. Going by herself was a bridge to the future, to letting go of the things that held her back.

The knowledge didn't keep him from worrying about her. He'd checked his watch a hundred times in the last two hours. How long did it take to say goodbye?

A lifetime, he thought.

He and Rose worked well together. He understood his parents working together all those years and loving each other. The Bachs were the same. He wondered if that could be said for Rose and him. He loved her. He wasn't sure if his mistrust had destroyed everything she felt for him.

David reached the employee entrance as Rose got there. He pulled the door open. Sunshine silhouetted her for a moment, turning her hair to a halo.

"Were you waiting here?" she asked.

"Not exactly. I saw your car from my window."

"Something must be wrong if you're waiting here."

"Nothing is wrong." They started walking toward her office.

"Everything is on schedule," David said. "Despite Mary's criminal activities, she was good at what she did."

"Then you came down here just to open the door for me?"

"I came down to make sure you were all right."

Rose blinked and looked at him. A second later her shoulders dropped. "Amber called you." She stated it as if she already knew the answer.

"She was concerned and couldn't get away."

"I didn't need any help," Rose said.

"That's what I told her. I knew if you went there alone, you needed to finish it without anyone there to hold your hand."

She looked at her hand. "You knew that?"

"I'm Dr. Phil, remember?" David said, trying to lighten the mood. "So, how did it go?"

"Well," she said. "I put the past behind me, if one can do that at will."

"It takes time."

"I know. The awful feelings that used to scare me when I thought of the house and the storm were gone. I looked at the empty lot and I know that things have changed. They are different and I can't go back and redo them. My only option is to go forward. And that's what I plan to do."

David smiled. He was unsure if he could say anything without showing her how much she meant to him. There had been a rift between them, and while he wanted her to know exactly how he felt, he needed to gauge her feelings.

"I didn't only come down to check on you," he said. "I wanted to apologize for all I did to lose your trust. I regret it and wish I could remove those words I said in anger. I know that's not possible."

"No, it's not possible."

David looked at her for some sign that she was kidding. Her mouth quivered and dissolved into a smile. Then a laugh.

Her teasing stopped as she looked in his eyes. "Kiss me," Rose said.

He didn't need to be asked twice. David had her in his arms at the speed of lightning. His mouth settled on hers and passion flowed between them. Heads bobbed back and forth. Arms entwined torso to torso. Fingers roamed over skin and fabric. He couldn't get enough of her. He could never get enough. She'd become part of his soul.

The kiss went on for an eternity before Rose came up for air. "We'd better get this party planned or there will be a lot of disappointed people. I know one with a new dress she's dying to wear."

"Amber?"

"And me."

"You'd be fine dressed in nothing," he teased, his own body stirring. "But if you choose to go that way, you'll never get out of the bedroom."

"We'd better go upstairs."

Or this might become a bedroom, David thought.

Once in the elevator, Rose became all business. "Have you restored my computer access?"

"Everything is up and running. And I apologize—"

"Stop," she interrupted. "We don't need to speak of

it again. We both did a lot of detecting and we found the moles. Let's go forward from here."

He liked that. David stepped toward her for a kiss when the doors opened.

Rose stopped in the doorway to her office. There was nothing personal in there since she'd never moved in. Her boxes from the old office were stacked near the desk as David had instructed Melanie to leave them. On the desk was a large arrangement of flowers. The office smelled of roses.

She went in and put her face in the bouquet, inhaling deeply. Then she pulled the card and read it. "'Roses for my Rose,'" she said, looking up at him.

"It's my last I'm-sorry gesture."

"Thank you. I love roses."

"David," someone called from the outer office.

"André! When did you get here?"

"It's a party, where else would I be?" his younger brother asked.

David was conflicted between wanting to be with Rose and spending the evening with his brother. He'd missed Rose during their absence and they'd just gotten back together. His family was due in tonight and they were all scheduled to go to dinner.

Timing was everything. If he had the chance, he'd stop the clock for everyone except the two of them. However, that wasn't within his power.

She came to the door. David introduced the two of them. "I suppose you two want to get out and see the beach before dark," Rose said. "I have some details to check off my list, so I'll see you tomorrow at the opening."

Not if he had anything to say about it, David thought. Dinner wasn't going to take all night. But what he had in mind just might.

Chapter 13

She knew he was going to come. Rose checked the last thing off her list at seven o'clock. She said good-night to the last of the craftsmen and department employees still there. They all went out together and got in their cars.

Rose had the gown she planned to wear the next day. The store would open for guests at five. She'd be there at three. But three o'clock was a day away. Before that David would come. He'd spent time with his family, but he'd whispered that he was coming by before morning. Rose was full of energy. She used the time to straighten the apartment. The boxes had been unpacked and the contents put in place.

Setting candles around the room, she lit several of them. She had a bottle of wine and two glasses cooling. When the knock came on the door, she rushed to open it.

"How was dinner?" she asked as soon as he came in.

"Long. All I could think of was you."

"Same here." Rose went to the table and pulled the bottle of wine out of the champagne bucket. She started to open it, but David came up behind her. His arms encircled her waist and he pulled her into his body. Rose had missed him, missed this. She leaned back, her hands covering his as their heads pressed together.

"I missed holding you," he said. "It kept me up nights."

"Me, too."

David's hands moved over her stomach. He ran them down her hips and around her behind. She felt sensations coursing through her. She felt as if a year had passed since she was in his arms. The burning began deep inside her. It was low but insistent. It promised something bigger, an explosion that wouldn't be tamped down.

She shuddered as his hands found her breasts. She let the wave of sensation lift her, turning her nipples into erotic nerves. He moved over them slowly, inciting arousal to the point that Rose bit her lower lip to keep from screaming. His head dropped to her neck and his mouth overwhelmed her senses. The heat was melting, and she loved it. Excitement ran through her like a fiery elixir. Craters vented their steam where his mouth sought her skin. Small moans of pleasure sounded deep in her throat. The more sound, the hotter the fire. Soon she didn't feel she could make any sound. Her throat would completely burn.

David's hands moved to her waist, spanning her body

as he ground his erection into her softness. Her legs went light and heavy at the same time. Guttural sounds came from him. Hungry sounds. Rose recognized them and knew their message. Heat pooled between her legs. Her arousal was complete. She didn't know if she could last much longer. David had the ability to make her forget all her thoughts, to focus only on him, on the genius of love, the joining of one man and one woman, on the pleasure that two people could bring to each other.

Rose trembled. She couldn't control it. She wanted him more than she wanted to breathe. David's hand moved with lightning speed. He turned her into his arms and like a heat-seeking missile his mouth found her. The wetness of his tongue was accepting and hungry. She wanted all of him. She took in the texture of his mouth, the feel of his hands on her, the length of his body—everything was magnified.

She needed him, wanted him, loved him. In her mind, she'd heard her declaration. They poured into each other, holding nothing back, giving and receiving with equal measure. This was their world, their place in the sun, their midnight madness. Everything that had happened to Rose took a back seat to the world she was in with David.

Rose wore a long shirt that stopped at her knees. Under it she wore nothing. David was intimately aware of that now. Reaching down, he crumpled the fabric, pulling it up until his fire-burning hands connected with her skin, bringing the fire to skin already liquefying.

Without asking, they began moving toward the bedroom. Their movements were like a dance. Their bodies stayed in contact, like flames moving in unison.

"You're beautiful," David whispered. His voice was strained. His hands followed her curves.

Rose wanted to see him, too. She pushed his clothes off, undressing him layer by layer. David let her. He seemed to like that she was taking control. Each time she looked up, his eyes were on her. They were passionate and hungry with desire. Rose never thought she could feel like this, wanting to love someone, wanting to give everything to another human being.

She felt lucky. Being pinned under that debris had brought him into her life. At the time she thought she would die, but if she had, Bach's would still be there and David would be in New York, never knowing the love he could have with her.

She nearly cried that the universe had brought them together, joined them, giving them the chance at something only they could create.

Completely naked, Rose looked at him. Her hands went to his chest and roamed over his skin. The feel of him excited her. Inside her own body, she could feel a change, a need that called to him, that said they had to come together. David took her head, his hands pushing into her hair as his mouth took hers. He angled her mouth. Her lips were soft against him, but seeking and wanting.

"I don't think I can stand this much longer," Rose moaned.

"You won't have to."

David sat on the bed, pulling her down with him.

Rose intentionally overbalanced, pushing him back and landing on top of him. Her legs between his, her arms around his neck, her body in tune with his.

Rose didn't wait for him to find a condom. She had one on her nightstand. Grabbing for it, she tore the packet and pulled out the rubber device.

Looking at him, she asked, "May I?"

He nodded.

He'd tortured her. Now it was her turn. She began at his shoulders, running her hands over shoulders that were more football player than counselor. She went down his arms, drawing her tongue over salty flesh until she reached his stomach. Her legs straddled him. His strong hands grasped her arms, holding on as he fought the need to take her immediately.

His erection stood up. Rose gathered the condom and covered him slowly, taking her time to pull the smooth rubber down the length of him. She felt him tense, his hands on her arms as the moans were forced from his throat.

He pulled her down, taking her mouth as he fit her body into his. Then with strong legs, he flipped her into position under him.

"That was awesome, and it's gonna cost you," he said.

She smiled.

With one knee he separated her legs and hovered over her before joining their two bodies in one movement. Their dance began, one that Rose wanted for life. She wanted to become familiar with everything about this ritual. She wanted it daily and nightly. She wanted to wake up with him each morning and go to bed each night, his arms holding her.

David pressed slowly into her, taking his time, keeping his need to plunge into her at bay. Rose pushed upward, taking him in, accommodating her body for his. As the strokes between them increased, as the fire they created grew hotter, so did the rhythm. Faster and faster he drove into her, increasing the pleasure with each tightening and relaxation of his legs.

She felt good, so good, too good. She didn't want this to end. She didn't ever want this to end. She worked harder, faster. Rose clamped her teeth shut. She wanted to scream. She could feel one coming from inside her, deep in her belly—it wanted release. Waves started in her stomach and fanned out, engulfing her entire body. From her navel to her fingernails, she felt every cell in her body retreat to one place, to one pleasure point, and David had found that point.

Their climax came on an unrestrained shout. They collapsed in a bath of sweat and entwined bodies. Rose took long inhales and exhales as she tried to get air into her lungs. She loved this man, this man who went to bat for her when she thought he didn't trust her, didn't believe her. How could she have been so undeserving? Rose kissed his shoulder, ran her hands over his slick body, loving the feel of him. If she had her way, she'd stay here for the rest of eternity.

The guests arrived like something out of a Hollywood opening. Limousines, black SUVs, classic cars, along with Toyotas, VWs and Chevrolets. The wealthy and the not so wealthy came out in their Sunday best. The Thorn family greeted them all warmly. David had her by his side even though it was outside of protocol for her to be there.

"We've broken so much protocol, what's another one?"

She laughed as his hand squeezed hers. Finally she had to move to see that everything was going well. The party planners needed her approval for certain emergencies. And Amber arrived on the arm of a man twice her age. He had gray temples and Rose wondered if he'd used an eraser to get that effect.

"Your gown is gorgeous," Rose said when they approached her. It was red with a square bodice and rhinestone straps. The front ended above her knees and the back flowed to the floor, showing off shoes that were encrusted with sequines and beads. Amber introduced her to Michael Sutton-Butler, a visitor from London who was in Logan Beach for the summer, teaching English literature at a local college.

"I hope you enjoy the beach," Rose told him.

"I love the warm weather," he responded.

Then Rose had to excuse herself to go put out another fire. On each of the eight shopping floors there was a different musical group. People gathered in places where they felt comfortable and looked around. Each one got tickets for games the planners had set up. People were joining in and seemed to be enjoying themselves.

"Having fun?" The whisper in her ear came from David. Rose could have smelled his cologne, but she

was so in tune with him that she could identify him
without seeing him.

"I'm having a wonderful time," she said.

"Come dance with me."

On the sixth floor was a small band that played popular music. David pulled her onto the dance floor and the
two of them got to hold each other in plain sight. Rose
saw David's two brothers watching them.

"Did I tell you how good you look in that dress?"

He swung her back and the dress swayed with the
movement of her steps. It was a regal purple, strap-
less gown. A short train ended the back and provided
a round back hem to the dress. Around her waist and
along the top were bands of Swarovski crystals. She
matched them with a silver rhinestone choker and a
pair of long crystal earrings. The see-through slippers
made her feel like Cinderella. But she had no intention
of leaving this ball without her prince.

"I love it," she said.

"And I'm going to love getting you out of it." David
pulled her close and swung her around, matching her
step for step.

"I think this dance is going to give your brothers
food for thought," she whispered.

David looked over her head at Blake and André
standing by one of the display cases filled with men's
ties.

"Shall we give them something to really talk about?"
David didn't wait for her to comply. He dipped his head
and kissed her on the mouth. She stood still, not running her arms up to his shoulders like she wanted to.

When he broke the kiss, he looked at his brothers, who both gave him a thumbs-up signal.

Rose and David laughed and continued dancing. Now she did run her hand up his arm and laid her head on his shoulder.

"I wish we could leave and go somewhere private," he whispered.

"What will your parents think?"

"Probably that I've taken you to bed?"

"David," she warned. "They wouldn't."

"No, they wouldn't," he said.

The music ended and Rose realized it was almost time for the Thorns to give their speech. She and David made their way to the ground floor. Rose moved to the side of the room. The family began taking up places by the back bank of elevators.

"Rose, everything looks wonderful. I love the displays," David's mother said as she stopped by on her way. "I'm so glad you're part of the team."

"Thank you," Rose murmured.

"Our son speaks highly of you," his father said.

"Not to mention what his brothers think," Blake added.

Rose looked from one brother to the other. Both appeared beside their mother. She wondered if they were going to play mischievous little boys and spill the news that David had kissed their Logan Beach assistant manager.

Neither of them did before the band played a few notes that got the crowd's attention. David stood in front of the band holding a microphone. He did the usual welcome speech, thanking everyone for coming, telling them that the doors would open promptly on Monday morning and joking that they should come and buy out the inventory.

"Speaking of inventory and every other aspect of the store, I'd like to introduce you to several people."

First, he introduced his parents, mentioning how his mother began the store and that she was making so much money that she needed to hire their dad. That got a laugh out of the group. His brothers were next, André in the New York store, and Blake in the San Francisco store. The twin cousins were absent. David explained they were at training seminars that they sorely needed. Again, laughter filtered through the crowd.

"This is our newest store, the House of Thorn Logan Beach. I was to be the manager here, but the family had an emergency board meeting last night and for the first time a House of Thorn store won't be run by a Thorn."

There was a collective intake of breath from the audience. Rose felt her body tense.

"We're turning over the manager's position of the Logan Beach store to Rosanna Turner." He extended his hand toward her. "Rose, would you join me?"

She was stunned. David had said nothing all through last night or today.

Amber was standing next to her. She took the glass Rose was holding and whispered, "No more than you deserve. Go get 'em."

As Rose made her way to the front, people applauded all around her. Tears welled in her eyes and she wiped them away. This was the last thing she expected. She got to the front and David took her hand. "Without Rose doing all the work, sometimes single-handedly directing everything you see or hear, she brings expertise from working in the former Bach's department store. If anyone deserves to manage this store, it's Ms. Turner."

Applause followed his comment.

"Now, if you wonder what this Thorn will be doing, I'm going to resume my law practice right here in Logan Beach."

The crowd applauded.

He turned to her. "Say a few words."

Rose took the microphone. And gave a welcome speech, thanking the Thorns for their belief in her. "And now, everyone, please enjoy the party."

David took her hand and they left the bandstand together.

"You two make a wonderful couple," Blake said, winking at her.

"Don't even think about it," David said.

"Think about what?" Blake said.

"About trying to get her away from me."

Rose smiled. She was enjoying this, but there were so many people vying for her attention that she needed to get away for a moment.

"May I have a sparkling water," she asked the bartender. He poured water into a glass, added a lemon peel and handed it to her.

"Congratulations," the bartender told her. "We're so glad a store is opening here again."

"Were you here before?" She didn't have to explain

what "before" meant. Anyone who lived in Logan Beach knew before meant before the storm.

"Yes, we were spared any damage, but there were so many we lost. The store will get things back on track."

"It will help. The building is fortified against storms. If we have another storm, make your way here. It's one of the safest places."

"I will, but I hope we never have another one."

Rose smiled. She got on the elevator and went to the third floor. The music being played on this floor was the "Wedding March" and other bridal music. From what Rose could see there were only a few people there. She needed a little quiet. David had totally surprised her. The Thorns were trusting her with the management. It was her dream. She thought it would be at Bach's, but this was good. They were both wonderful stores. This was a better store. As she'd just explained to the bartender.

Rose walked into the space where the gowns hung. The area had been set up with a small aisle, so the bride could see herself walking down it. Rose sidestepped it, resisting the urge to pretend to be a bride. Her purple gown was in sharp contrast to all the white around her. Going toward one of the display cases, she smiled at the oversized portrait behind it. On the wall hung a huge photo of a smiling bride. She'd just come out of a church and the guests threw rice at her. Her head was up and a huge smile graced her face. Rose loved that photo.

"I thought I'd find you here." David's voice came from behind her. "Our new manager."

Rose swung around. She wanted to fly down the aisle and into his arms.

"David, are you sure?" she asked. "I'm so afraid this is a dream."

"You earned it," he said.

"How did you know I'd be here?"

"This is your favorite floor," he said.

Rose was surprised that he knew that. She remembered Amber telling her that he knew how she liked her coffee. David took in details about her that no one else had.

"Were you looking for me?" Rose asked.

"I did have one more question to ask you before we go back to the party."

"What's that?"

"Come here, I want to show you this first."

Rose went to him. He stood in front of the display case that held gloves, bridal bags with beads on them and... Rose looked down. She moved her face closer to the glass.

"What's that?"

"Something I thought was a perfect accessory, but as the store manager you have the last say about it."

David moved around and opened the case. He took the item out and set it on the counter for her to see.

"Is that...?" She couldn't finish the sentence.

"It's a Rosanna diamond. I had it specially cut for you."

"Me?"

"It goes with the question." David picked up the box

and pulled the ring free of its velvet background. "Will you marry me?"

Rose's hand went to her stomach. "So many changes in one day."

"Good changes. You deserve them." He looked at her. "It will be a good change for me, too. I love you. I've loved you for a really long time."

"I love you, too."

"Then you'll marry me?"

"Yes," she said. "Yes." She repeated it several times, until David slipped the ring on her finger and came around to close her repeating words with a kiss.

"I love you," she said when he lifted his mouth. "I've wanted to tell you for weeks, but the time never was right," she said.

"From now on, it will always be right."

She put her head on his shoulder. "Do you think we should return to the party?"

"Not yet, this is our party. Let's stay for just a few more minutes."

Rose laughed suddenly.

"What's so funny?"

She spread her hand out, looking at the ring. "I was thinking about what Amber will do when I tell her. She'll probably go into wedding mode and we'll have everyone from the US Navy to the red caps at the airport in attendance."

"Wait until my mother hears. Her firstborn getting married to a woman who has no mother to plan her wedding. This might be our last silent moment together until the honeymoon."

Rose laughed. She was deliriously happy. Before she met David, she thought her life was over, that there would never again be any light in it.

And now she no longer looked at her life as before the storm and after it. David had changed everything and she would always love him.

She curled into his arms, clinging close to him and humming the "Wedding March."

* * * * *

If you liked this story, pick up these titles from Shirley Hailstock's WEDDINGS BY DIANA *series:*

HIS LOVE MATCH
SOMEONE LIKE YOU
ALL HE NEEDS

Available now from Harlequin Kimani Romance!

COMING NEXT MONTH
Available September 26, 2017

#541 NEVER CHRISTMAS WITHOUT YOU
by Nana Malone and Reese Ryan
This collection features two sizzling holiday stories from fan-favorite authors. Unwrap the ultimate gift of romance as two couples explore the magic of true love at Christmas.

#542 TEMPTED AT TWILIGHT
Tropical Destiny • **by Jamie Pope**
Nothing fires up trauma surgeon Elias Bradley like the risk of thrilling adventure. But when he meets Dr. Cricket Warren, she awakens emotions that take him by surprise. And now she's having his baby… He's ready to step up, but can they turn a fantasy into a lifetime of romance?

#543 THE HEAT BETWEEN US
Southern Loving • **by Cheris Hodges**
Appointed to head Atlanta's first-ever jazz festival, marketing guru Michael "MJ" Jane sets out to create an annual event to rival New Orleans. Even if that means hiring her crush and former marine Jamal Carver to run security. Can love keep Jamal and MJ in harmony…forever?

#544 SIZZLING DESIRE
Love on Fire • **by Kayla Perrin**
Lorraine Mitchell cannot forget her heated encounter with firefighter Hunter Holland. Weeks later, she is stunned to discover that his father—a former patient of hers—has left her a large bequest! Despite mutual mistrust, reviving their spark might ignite a love that's as deep as it is scorching…

Get 2 Free Books,
Plus 2 Free Gifts—
just for trying the
Reader Service!

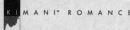

SPECIAL EXCERPT FROM

Flirting with a gorgeous stranger at the bar is how Lorraine Mitchell celebrates her longed-for newly single status. One-night stands usually run hot and wild before quickly flaming out, but Lorraine cannot forget her heated encounter with firefighter Hunter Holland. And reviving their spark just might ignite a love that's as deep and true as it is scorching...

Read on for a sneak peek at
SIZZLING DESIRE,
the next exciting installment in author
*Keyla Perrin's **LOVE ON FIRE** series!*

"You know why I'm here tonight," Lorraine said to Hunter as they neared the bar. "What brings you here?"

"I'm new in town," Hunter explained.

"Aah. Are you new to California?" Lorraine asked. "Did you move here from another state?"

"I did, yes. But I'm not new to Ocean City. I grew up here, then moved to Reno when I hit eighteen. I lived and worked there for sixteen years, and now I'm back. I'm a firefighter."

That explained why he was in such good shape. Firefighters were strong, their bodies immaculately honed in order to be able to rescue people from burning buildings and other disastrous situations. No wonder he had come to her aid in such a chivalrous way.

She swayed a little—deliberately—so she could wrap her fingers tighter around his arm. Yes, she was shamelessly copping a feel. She barely even recognized herself.

"Oops," Hunter said, securing his hand on her back to make sure she was steady. "You okay?"

"I'm fine," Lorraine said. "You're so sweet." *And so hot.*

So hot that she wanted to smooth her hands over his muscular pecs for a few glorious minutes.

She turned away from him and continued toward the bar. What was going on with her? It must be the alcohol making her react so strongly to this man.

Though the truth was, she didn't care what was bringing out this reaction in her. Because every time Hunter looked at her, she felt incredibly desirable—something she hadn't felt with Paul since the early days of their marriage. But unlike her ex-husband, Hunter's attraction for her was obvious in that dark, intense gaze. Every time their eyes connected, the chemistry sizzled.

Lorraine's heart was pounding with excitement, and it was a wonderful feeling after all the pain and heartache she'd gone through recently. It was nice to feel the pitter-patter of her pulse because of a guy who rated eleven out of ten on the sexy scale.

Lorraine veered to the left to sidestep a group of women. And all of a sudden, her heel twisted beneath her body. This time, she started to go down in earnest. Hunter quickly swooped his arms around her, and the next thing she knew, he was scooping her into his arms.

"Oh, my God," she uttered. "You're not carrying me—"

Don't miss SIZZLING DESIRE
by Kayla Perrin, available October 2017
wherever Harlequin® Kimani Romance™
books and ebooks are sold!

LOVE
Harlequin
romance?

Join our Harlequin community to share your thoughts and connect with other romance readers!

Be the first to find out about promotions, news, and exclusive content!

Sign up for the Harlequin e-newsletter and download a free book from any series at

www.TryHarlequin.com

CONNECT WITH US AT:

Harlequin.com/Community

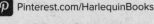 Facebook.com/HarlequinBooks

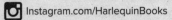 Twitter.com/HarlequinBooks

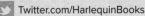 Instagram.com/HarlequinBooks

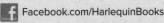 Pinterest.com/HarlequinBooks

ReaderService.com

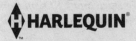 **HARLEQUIN**®

**ROMANCE WHEN
YOU NEED IT**

HSOCIAL2017

Want to give in to temptation with
steamy tales of irresistible desire?

Check out **Harlequin® Presents®**,
Harlequin® Desire and
Harlequin® Kimani™ Romance books!

New books available every month!

CONNECT WITH US AT:

Harlequin.com/Community

 Facebook.com/HarlequinBooks

 Twitter.com/HarlequinBooks

 Instagram.com/HarlequinBooks

 Pinterest.com/HarlequinBooks

ReaderService.com

**ROMANCE WHEN
YOU NEED IT**

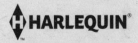